JOSEPH WALSER'S MACHINE

OTHER WORKS BY GONÇALO M. TAVARES IN ENGLISH TRANSLATION

Jerusalem

Learning to Pray in the Age of Technique

JOSEPH WALSER'S MACHINE

Gonçalo M. Tavares

Translated by Rhett McNeil

DALKEY ARCHIVE PRESS
CHAMPAIGN / DUBLIN / LONDON

Originally published in Portuguese as *A máquina de Joseph Walser* by Editorial Caminho,
Lisbon, 2004
Copyright © Gonçalo M. Tavares, 2003 by arrangement with Literarische Agentur Mertin Inh.
Nicole Witt e. K., Frankfurt am Main, Germany
Translation and introduction copyright © 2012 by Rhett McNeil
First Edition, 2012
All rights reserved

Library of Congress Cataloging-in-Publication Data

Tavares, Gonçalo M., 1970-
[Maquina de Joseph Walser. English]
Joseph Walser's machine / Goncalo M. Tavares ; translated by Rhett McNeil. -- 1st ed.
p. cm.
"Originally published in Portuguese as A maquina de Joseph Walser by Editorial Caminho,
Lisbon, 2004"--T.p. verso.
Includes bibliographical references and index.
ISBN 978-1-56478-677-7 (pbk. : alk. paper)
I. McNeil, Rhett. II. Title.
PQ9282.A89M3713 2009
869.3'5--dc23
2011025604

Partially funded by a grant from the Illinois Arts Council, a state agency, and by the University
of Illinois at Urbana-Champaign

The publication of this book was partly supported by the DGLB—Direcção-Geral do Livro e
das Bibliotecas / Portugal

www.dalkeyarchive.com

Cover: design and composition by Danielle Dutton, illustration by Nicholas Motte
Printed on permanent/durable acid-free paper and bound in the United States of America

The shock of the similar . . .

—MARIA FILOMENA MOLDER

He wanted to say the Lord's Prayer, but all he could remember was his multiplication tables.

—HANS CHRISTIAN ANDERSEN

TRANSLATOR'S INTRODUCTION

Joseph Walser's Machine (2004) is the second book in Gonçalo
M. Tavares's series "The Kingdom": four novels connected by a
handful of overlapping characters, a number of recurring themes,
and, perhaps most importantly, a strikingly odd style. The third
novel in the series, *Jerusalem*, was awarded the prestigious Saramago Prize in Portugal, and the final novel, *Learning to Pray in
the Age of Technique*, was recently awarded the prize for Best Foreign Book in France, which has only ever been awarded to one
other Portuguese-language novelist, António Lobo Antunes in
1997. Tavares's work has also been championed by the old guard
of European novelists, including Jacques Roubaud, who read his
own translation of Tavares's stories in an Oulipo meeting, and José
Saramago, who heaped hyperbolic praise on the younger writer,
stating that in the history of the novel in Portugal there is very
much "a before and after Gonçalo M. Tavares."

The novels in "The Kingdom" series are all set in an unnamed
European city filled with streets and characters with vaguely Ger-

manic-sounding names. Within this hazily defined setting, Tavares's narrators and characters grapple with fundamental questions of human existence (the relationship between humanity and the material world, the behavior of humankind when faced with war, sickness, and death) as well the language with which to express or examine these questions. Indeed, the third-person narrative voice in Tavares's "Kingdom" novels is unceasingly self-reflexive, wrestling with language in order to describe both simple actions and complex, often paradoxical philosophical notions. As such, the prose in *Joseph Walser's Machine* is consistently jarring, abounding with bizarre turns of phrase and circumlocutions. The description of Joseph Walser's prized collection could serve as well as a description of the narrative voice of Tavares's novels: "This world which, when viewed from the outside, might seem illogical and strange, was in fact thoroughly ordered; it was a secondary order, one that only Walser could perceive." The order in Tavares's books is a bizarre order, a seemingly "illogical and strange" order, but an order nonetheless.

Throughout the novel, Tavares's narrator describes objects, actions, feelings, and concepts as if they were newly formed, with measurable qualities and definable characteristics, yet without names or rote phrases to accompany them. As such, we end up with descriptions of wartime that eschew terms like "bullet" or "shrapnel," as in the following passage: "a few hearts pierced by shiny pieces of metal, damned by a material that is far from useless in war: a dense substance incompatible with life." At other points in the novel, the narrator refuses to name a concept until after the peculiar particularities of it have been articulated, as in this strange description of an idea as commonplace as "weekend fun": "Saturday night the city takes on an odd logic; a schizoid personality becomes readily apparent in men who are able to move straight from their loathsome days into occupying themselves, remorselessly, with nonstop dancing and dim, arousing lights. People are having fun." There is a cool, almost scientific detachment in this sort of prose, as if the narrator were examining human behavior for the first time, without the linguistic baggage and habitual terms and phrases bequeathed by the history of a language. The narrative voice is free of ready-made opinion or moralizing, for certain, but it is also free of that which many readers and all nonreaders demand from their books: instantaneous intelligibility.

Tavares's evasive narrative strategies call to mind what Viktor Shklovsky says about Tolstoy in *Theory of Prose*. Shklovsky argues that everyday language tends toward the routine, the clichéd, the automatic, and that the function of art is to force us to see with fresh eyes, to "return sensation to our limbs." To that end, Tolstoy employed a strategy that Shklovsky calls "enstrangement," through which he forced the reader to hear language anew, to be jarred into consciousness by poetic language, which subverts and distorts and destroys automatic, everyday language. Shklovsky then goes on to describe a method of enstrangement utilized by Tolstoy that could equally be used to characterize the narration in *Joseph Walser's Machine*: "[H]e does not call a thing by its name, that is, he describes it as if it were perceived for the first time, while an incident is described as if it were happening for the first time." In the world of Tavares's novel, such historically and politically loaded topics as war, military occupation, violence, and death are described as if they were occurring for the first time, divorced from both their historical resonances and their usual linguistic milieus. As such, the narrator struggles to find the precise terms, phrases, or metaphors to describe the action of the novel, at times expounding at length about a strange new combination of adjective and noun, at others practically giving up on the possibility of language to reveal or convey meaning, as in this one-off description of the tempo of war: "The war continued apace: like a lunatic, or maybe like some other thing." Tavares's prose refuses to follow the smooth, automatic routes of everyday speech, instead opting for the more treacherous terrain of new poetic formulation. Shklovsky's definition of poetry—which included literary prose as well—is a concise description of Tavares's narrative style: "impeded, distorted speech."

Translating Gonçalo M. Tavares, therefore, is an exercise in resisting temptation, the oddly persistent temptation of clear, everyday language. The "impeded, distorted" prose of the "Kingdom" novels puts the translator in a tough spot, stuck between the Scylla of the near-sacred original text and the Charybdis of the eventual thoughtful reader. On the one hand, the translator reveres the original text and its uniquely stilted inner weave, and on the other, she looks forward to the promised reader, who, at long last, will justify the book. There is an impulse on the part of the translator to coddle the reader, a temptation to smooth over the very elements that make the book bizarre or original, those elements that would restore the reader to her senses. With Tavares, the temptation is to convert such odd turns of phrase as "a few hearts pierced by shiny pieces of metal, damned by a material that is far from useless in war: a dense substance incompatible with life" to something more palatable, more automatic, like "a shiny piece of shrapnel, a valuable tool in wartime." Or convert "a dense substance that is incompatible with life" into "bullets, which take human lives." Yet giving into the temptation to render Tavares's prose in the automatic English that would set a reader's mind at ease would be at once to obliterate the nuance of the original text and to do a disservice to the reader, preventing her from experiencing the wholly new sensation of this strange book. It is the translator's duty to resist this temptation, especially in the case of those sorts of books we call literary, avant-garde, or subversive, whose value lies precisely in their transgression of aesthetic and linguistic norms.

RHETT MCNEIL

2012

JOSEPH WALSER'S MACHINE

PART I

CHAPTER I

1

He was a strange man, and his wife couldn't help but laugh as she listened to him. As if humans were "substances that thought," Joseph Walser had said. Of course humans are *substances that think*! Substances with souls, as Margha would put it.

Joseph Walser headed to his room. Margha didn't even look up.

Walser was a collector. Of what? It's too early to say. But on this morning he had significantly expanded his collection.

He wore a simple pair of pants, almost like a peasant's, and his hazel-colored shoes were absolutely out of style.

His wife said: "You're dressed like you're from another century. No one thinks that way anymore."

2

Joseph Walser doesn't have his papers on him.

Someone says: "No messing around these days, you always have to have your papers."

Joseph Walser receives this reprimand in silence.

Distance was proportional to astonishment. When events took place just a few inches or feet away: no big deal, just monotony. Monotony exists in close proximity to mankind, while astonishing things are always out of reach.

The introduction of a single new element into a peaceful environment can effect radical changes in one's outlook for the day to come. Death had not yet been introduced as an everyday element, but this next month was going to be tough, vile even, according to some forecasts.

"A vile month," murmured Walser to his wife Margha.

But a month one can't avoid touching. Relegating all your humiliating fears to the tips of your fingers.

You'll touch the next month the way you touch the water of a dirty river with your right hand: afterward you have to clean your fingers, you have to wash them.

The technique of influencing men by frightening them about things that don't exist yet is ancient. It's happening once again, now. There's talk of a military unit approaching with great appetite; that's the word they use: appetite. As if weapons had stomachs, the way organisms do. And a sort of grotesque, metallic saliva. However, mental processes are the only things that have been disturbed, thus far; the physical reality of things still remains calm and well-organized. Factories are keeping up the diligent commotion that corresponds to the routine movements of their peaceful machines, and the necessary products subsequently materialize. In industry, the phenomenon of cause and effect is sustained, and none of the machines interrupt their customary processes to veer off toward such things as miracles or explosions.

"Fortunately, no miracles," mutters Klober Muller, the foreman at the factory where Joseph Walser works.

As if war were just an excessive concentration of miracles. An irritating series of such occurrences taking place over the shortest possible period of time, a supernatural acceleration, a feat of pure human arrogance, and—more than mere impropriety—a crude domination over time.

There need to be significant pauses in between events. "They shouldn't just pile up like a heap of shoddy merchandise, events aren't shoddy merchandise, they're valuable things," said Klober.

Joseph Walser was standing next to him, in his hazel-colored shoes, which were absolutely out of style.

Klober couldn't help but notice.

"Those shoes of yours," he said, "are absolutely irresponsible."

Joseph Walser looked down at his own shoes and then raised his head back up. The smile that he thought of affecting in that fleetingly tense moment disappeared when his eyes took in the expression on Klober's face. The foreman wasn't kidding. Not at all: he was annoyed.

"Your shoes are absolutely irresponsible," repeated Klober Muller.

3

"No one wears shoes like that anymore."

How many times had Joseph Walser heard that phrase in the last two weeks? What was going on? He had worn these shoes, or similar ones, for years. No one had ever bothered him about them before. No one had ever before cared about his shoes in the least, neither their color nor shape. Why now?

"I don't care about your shoes or your ideas, do you understand, my dear Walser? What I told you yesterday isn't important to me, but it is extremely important to you. Can you see the difference? Can you see the difference that exists between the two of us? Between my shoes and your shoes, between my ideas and your ideas? I'm not interested in your shoes and I'm not interested in your ideas. But you're interested in my ideas; that's the difference between us, you see?

"As for your shoes, I've already forgotten about them. It's true that your shoes are absolutely irresponsible, yes, I said it, and I'll say it again. You might want an explanation, but I won't give it to you. You should just figure it out. It's your duty. Mr. Joseph Walser should learn to pick up on things without needing an explanation. There's an army approaching, and you want explanations about your shoes?

"But I'll explain what I can to you, Walser. A vile month is coming, as they've said on the news, and you, my friend, are wearing dirty, worn-out shoes, you see? You should clean them immediately. We must fight filth with hygiene or we'll be defeated, don't you see, dear Walser?

"Order is more important every day. I'm shocked that you still haven't noticed this.

"Organized insanity is approaching and we'll have to confront it with calm. No one respects hysteria. War makes insanity look ridiculous. Order, my dear Walser.

"Outright hysteria and a mere untucked shirt should be thought of as belonging to the same universe: the universe of disorder. You can't confront collective insanity with your shirt untucked—do you get it, Joseph Walser?"

4

"The machines of war are on their way, but don't be afraid. The machines approaching the city aren't the problem: it's the machines that are already here.

"Multiple generations of machines, their History, Walser: they progress. Just like our ideas. But machines become autonomous, ideas don't.

"Machines already play a part in the country's History, as well as our individual biographies. They don't just have a material or factual trajectory. They also have a History of the spirit, a pathway that has been traced in the world of the invisible, in the world of that which is felt and thought. It is even believed that machines are guiding Man to regions that are closer to Truth.

"And joy, as well, can be reduced to a binary system. To a *yes* or a *no*, a 0 or a 1: it exists or doesn't exist. And this effectiveness, my dear Walser, this fundamental effectiveness, this primary effectiveness, already depends, in large part, upon machines, upon the swiftness with which they transform causes and necessities into beneficial effects. Happiness has already been reduced to a system that machines can comprehend, and in which they can participate and intervene. At this point in time there is no individual happiness that remains independent from technology, Walser, my friend. If you want exact numbers, we can throw some exact numbers around: individual happiness on a given day is, who knows, 70% dependent on the material effectiveness of machines. The fact that one's invisible happiness is at the mercy of one's concrete happiness, a happiness of substances in dialogue with one another, of metal pieces that fit neatly into each other and solve problems by repeating certain tasks, all this may seem strange; but such is the century in which we live.

"Being happy no longer depends on the things that we commonly associate with the word Spirit. It depends on concrete substances. Human happiness is a mechanism."

5

"Look at this factory: we're in the presence of a supernatural wonder. Everything is so stupidly predictable with these machines that it becomes surprising; it's the great wonder of the century, the great surprise: we were able to achieve the exact thing that we wanted to happen. We've made the future redundant, and therein lies the danger.

"If individual happiness depends on these mechanisms and also becomes predictable, existence itself will, therefore, be redundant and unnecessary: there will be no expectations, struggles, or apprehensions.

"They speak of machines of war, but there is no such thing as a peaceful machine, Walser."

CHAPTER II

1

Joseph Walser lived a disciplined life. He awoke at seven o'clock, shaved, and ate a quick breakfast. At eight thirty he entered the factory that belonged to the empire of Leo Vast, the most important businessman in the city, whom Joseph Walser, in ten years of employment, had only seen twice, and only from far away.

He ate lunch from one to two. At six in the evening he left the factory and returned home, on foot.

Margha Walser always greeted her husband with a peck on the cheek. They didn't have any children, their days were quiet, and the discussions between them were respectful.

Margha was concerned about the way her husband dressed. It wasn't just the shoes; his whole wardrobe was ancient, unfashionable, disheveled. They weren't excessively poor; Joseph couldn't afford to buy expensive clothes, to be sure, but it was clear that his slovenliness wasn't due to any mere financial constraint.

Joseph Walser was a strange man, and he seldom spoke. The carelessness in his manner of dress was nothing more than the reflection of his carelessness in relation to the outside world. He listened much more than he spoke, even with his wife; however, the way he listened sometimes irritated his interlocutor:

"My dear Joseph Walser, are you really listening to me?" was asked of him countless times.

Walser's face bespoke a constant, general state of alienation. As though his life was unfolding internally, not in the world around him. As though Walser's days were much more complicated inside his head, and this internal existence required greater attention than his concrete, external tasks.

There was only one situation in which he felt completely given over to the world outside: when he was operating "his" machine in the factory. This intense concentration wasn't, however, a personal choice, but rather something inherent to the danger of this machine: any distraction could cause an accident with serious consequences.

There had already been a number of accidents among his colleagues. One of them fatal. Everyone agreed that it was a terrible risk, that a number of relatively implausible probabilities had all been combined, such that the improbable was no longer improbable, and a few years back had become fact: the type of machine that Joseph Walser operated had caused a death.

Thus, it required of him an unceasing attention. A precise attention, as Klober always put it, stressing the strangeness of combining such a vast and unknowable word like "attention" with a firm and wholly unequivocal word like "precision." *Precise attention* was essential in the person operating this machine. Attention defined as an emotional characteristic, rather than simply a bodily or manual one, said Klober, adding in the operative word: precision. A rational word, from the world of the sciences.

In front of that machine, it wasn't enough to be attentive the way any given animal is generally attentive; it was necessary to be attentive in a precise manner, in a manner of which only humans are capable. Precision, said Klober, is a word that only exists and makes sense when it is used with regard to humans. No other creature has science, or gives it any importance.

The term "precise attention" summed up what was necessary in Joseph Walser's job: to be a perfect animal, an unpredictable and non-animalistic animal, an organism without instability, an organism able to maintain a consistent, immutable identity in front of the machine. For that machine required of every one of the workers a set of fixed, repeated movements, performed in a predetermined sequence. Any deviation from these precise movements, these movements that were the product of precise attention, any deviation at all would result in a disruption of the machine's efficiency and, therefore, a smaller output—or even a breakdown.

Walser had long since operated the machine with an unceasing concentration, since, from the beginning, he'd realized the following: if the machine could, in the worst case, as a result of a mistake, kill him, him the honorable citizen Joseph Walser, in peacetime, this most tranquil of times, while lazy children played in the parks on Sundays, then he, Joseph Walser, was, after all, at war, for he was dealing with a dangerous friend, a friend that was potentially an enemy, a mortal enemy, because it could—not in a few months or a couple of days, but in a second—turn into *that which seeks to inflict bodily harm*. The foundation of his very existence—this machine—which supported his family and was, therefore, what saved him, day after day, from being some other person, eventually his own negative, the opposite of the Man that he thought himself to be; this machine saved him, perhaps, from the fate of becoming a bum, or someone who nurtures a categorical hatred for his fellow man; but in saving him day after day, the machine also constantly threatened him, without abeyance. A mistake with the machine that saved him so *monotonously* could, from one moment to the next, put an end to his life, or at least to the interrelation between his body and his life.

Thus, Joseph Walser was constantly face-to-face with an enemy. But by being proficient and by maintaining his precise attention at every moment, Joseph was able, day after day, year after year, to keep this enemy at enough of a distance that he ended up considering it a friend.

Joseph Walser loved his machine, but he knew that his machine hated him, the human, so much that it never let him out of its sight; the machine was watching him constantly, looking for a mistake, hoping for a mistake.

In fact, Joseph Walser could feel that the machine, *his* machine, was watching him. The hierarchical relationship between these two entities was clear to him: the machine belonged to a superior tier: it could save him or destroy him; it could make it so that his life went on repeating itself, almost infinitely, or it could, on the other hand, from one moment to the next, produce a sudden change. Joseph Walser never understood his role as employee and his subservient role with regard to the outside world better than when he was face-to-face with his machine, in the full performance of his duties. The subservience that could be discerned in Walser when talking with Klober, the foreman, was absolutely insignificant compared to the subservience he displayed while at work, leaning against his machine, hugging it or battling against it (depending on the point of view). The outside world never dominated him so completely, and his energy was never so entirely directed outward, as they were in this situation.

He had heard this complaint from his wife, from the foreman, and even from people higher up in the hierarchy, but he never allowed, or—better said—never succumbed to the error, the dangerous error, of inattention and carelessness in front of his machine; he couldn't let "his" machine ever ask him, as the others had: "My dear Joseph Walser, are you really listening to me?"

2

Given the nature of his work and the dangerous machine with which he contended, Joseph Walser didn't need any additional intensity in his life. He viewed the start of the war and the invasion of the city as almost dull. He didn't perceive the beginning of hostilities as a novelty, but just one more repetition. The sensation of continuity through time was, in fact, indestructible for Walser, in spite of the commotion in the sky, which heralded the arrival of new airborne machines and animosities. Peacetime flows seamlessly into wartime and the new wartime will later flow seamlessly into a new peacetime. And nothing is interrupted. Nothing fundamental. A person isn't interrupted by war, there are no interruptions at all: he is always Man, there's no one else, there's no 2nd Man, there's only one, the 1st, and he's the one—the same one from centuries earlier, and he'll be the same one in the future— the one who lives through everything in a state of boredom, even through war. Monotony and indifference.

Human existence, at its most essential, hadn't been the least bit upset after thirty centuries and three thousand violent conflicts. If what you want is to change the order of existence, it's clear that war won't do, Walser had heard from Klober, the foreman.

But peace can't change Man either, of course. The dice were already rolled long ago.

CHAPTER III

1

Joseph Walser went out every Saturday night to Fluzst M.'s house, where he played dice for low-stakes bets with three other work-mates. The five men all worked at the same factory. They were all low-level employees and made average wages. Over the years their passion for games of chance had brought them together. There was no exceptional friendship among them, but they rarely missed a Saturday. The amounts being bet in the game could be considered small, when compared with other underground games around the city, but in proportion to their wages the amounts were large. All five men were married; for the players, their wives were the most difficult thing about their gambling. There wasn't a single wife who didn't complain about her husband losing a certain amount of money in the game.

Each week, one of the five men was allowed to bring a guest to the game. Thus, every five weeks it was Joseph Walser's turn to bring a guest, if he wanted to; but it never happened.

Having dice in one's hand simplified the world.

Life was reduced to six numbers, embedded in each die, as if the die were not merely an object belonging to a game of chance, but some concrete substance with the ability to produce a formula that could explain all the interconnected forces on earth.

During those moments, another kind of decision-making was required, different from the kind that the passing days normally require of each man. The tension that results from having an infinite number of possibilities evaporated; there, on that table, each of the dice limited the number of possible pathways. And what pleased Joseph Walser was precisely the sensation that at that table, at long last, there were limits. There were no unknown elements, there was no annoying "something else" that could pop up, or indeed anything unseen. There was nothing lacking, everything was there already, in the game, nothing new could crop up to disrupt the proceedings. There were six numbers stuck to the die and they weren't going anywhere. There was no seventh cipher, no seventh hypothesis. Six was the limit.

It was this precision that excited him, this precision that was well-defined by immutable limits that, nonetheless, allowed room for his peculiar decisions, which, in truth, were not decisions at all. Just like everybody else, Walser accepted what the dice gave him. He accepted the decisions the dice made. The one great decision in the game was, at root, the profound and powerful decision to accept, the decision that one is ready for absolute submission, willing not to interfere in the events taking place. He accepted his position as something exterior to these events and rolled the dice. Thus, Joseph Walser's big decision was made a few hours before each game began.

When, after a few minutes of hesitation, he stood up each Saturday, left his house, and walked through the streets—his pace not too fast and not too slow—towards Fluzst's house, it was clear, indeed, that he had already made his big decision: he was going to play.

Because it was obvious that the dice themselves were more powerful than the players. These men were used to obeying during the week, and on Saturday, oddly enough, they entered into another system of obedience: that of luck, chance.

It would be quite another thing if Joseph Walser entertained himself playing games of skill, in which individual ability determined victory or defeat. For example, the shooting games they have at the little fair in the city. There were many men, including some of their workmates, who went out to the fair on Saturday nights to show off their athletic prowess and ingenuity; accomplishments that they would later take great pride in, during the following week.

But how could a man take pride in his luck? How could he take pride in a mere *apparition* (each spotted side that emerged face up *appeared* almost by surprise)? In spite of the limited number of possible outcomes, the players shouted in amazement every time the dice came to a stop.

Those five men were, therefore, face-to-face with apparitions, apparitions of luck or of chance, of high numbers and low numbers. Apparitions, things that emerged into the world without any cause, things that were separated from the rest of the universe because they were purely effects, with no antecedents, no logic, no law: the players tossed the dice on the table and the results appeared. Like ghosts, Joseph said one time.

2

But there was an immediate physical pleasure just before these apparitions came into being. Right at the moment that Joseph Walser picked up the two dice and rattled them around in his hand, feeling like a cook mixing two ingredients.

Joseph Walser's right hand formed a shell where he stowed the dice; one could call it a cavern, sheltering two similar animals—but motionless, unbreathing animals, and the only sound emerging from the cavern is a consequence of their getting knocked against each other, achieved by the movements of the central fingers on Joseph Walser's right hand in concert with his thumb.

At the very moment he handled the dice before throwing them down on the table, Walser felt an inexplicable excitement, a feeling he couldn't quite classify. At that moment he concentrated on images from the past, or even invented images, in which parts of the anatomy of young women seemed to merge somehow with the dots that represented numbers on each side of the cubes. This perverse contamination of the dice by such specific images of the human body elicited a somewhat confused image in Walser's mind, but it was expressed externally by a smile that the other men at the table couldn't characterize as anything less than obscene. Walser experienced—at the moment when his thumb, index, and other fingers rolled the dice around on the palm of his closed hand—a feeling of control that didn't exist in any other circumstances in his life. In that instant Walser felt that he was in control of the world, that he was manipulating it, that he was capable of making it say *yes* or *no* with only a quick change in the movement of one of his fingers. As if, at that moment, the yes or no of the physical world depended exclusively on the angle of his thumb.

However, on that night Joseph Walser decided to walk out on the game after only an hour.

"We're just getting started," said Fluzst, but Walser settled up and said good night.

Without knowing why. He felt uneasy.

3

It wasn't the war; he had decided to stay neutral some time ago. An army had already invaded the city, but that wasn't any of his business. He viewed the war as though it were a science that he didn't understand: he couldn't see what it was, didn't understand its methods, its strategies, its system for taking measurements. I shouldn't make statements about something I don't understand, much less act on something I don't understand, Walser himself had said. That which one does not understand should only be observed. Nothing more.

War was a science that used obscure terminology, and since he felt timid and never intruded into conversations about topics he didn't understand, he had decided not to meddle with it. The factory where he worked was still operating as usual, his position at work was secure, he hadn't been switched over to a different task, he hadn't even had to change so much as the smallest of his movements in the operation of his machine; hence, everything was still the same.

He also hadn't stopped collecting. His secret collection continued to grow, and now, after a few tanks and other military machines had entered the city, there were possibilities for his collection to become even more unusual.

Everything was undisturbed, his life was still intact, inalterable. The vile month that was foreseen had never arrived, or else it had arrived, but never came near Walser's life. If I don't understand this vileness, if I can't identify it, if I don't pay attention to its language, then I remain clean. And Walser felt clean.

On that night, his fellow players had spoken of a horse that had been lying in the middle of the road, dead, for days, decomposing more and more, yet, even so, Walser wasn't even curious enough to ask which road it was on. He merely hoped that he would chance to walk by it, and that was that.

His uneasiness, however, had passed. It was ten thirty, and since he never went home before midnight, it was as if he were just out for a stroll, without any need to hurry, taking slow steps, feeling perfectly safe, despite the rumors of violence in some parts of the city. He was much too insignificant for anyone to come after him, for anyone to be violent with him. No one is going to direct their violence at a man like me, thought Walser, and he felt more pride than shame in this. He was taking a peaceful walk at night without any fear, without anyone bothering him. What more could he want?

Suddenly, Joseph Walser saw a woman emerge from one of the houses, taking tiny, but very quick, steps down the road, and wearing a coat that almost covered her face.

Joseph Walser stood with his hands in his pockets, alone, and smiled: "One more case of adultery," he said under his breath. But the smile soon disappeared: Walser looked attentively at the bulky figure heading, quickly and guiltily, down the street. He recognized the coat, recognized the shoes: it was his wife.

CHAPTER IV

1

He didn't want to go home right away. He had time and wanted to think.

Joseph Walser was now walking at a different pace, but he hadn't stopped for a single minute. His wife would already be home, sure enough. He looked around: he had just come to some streets that he didn't know too well. He turned back. He wanted to see the house that his wife had come from.

He was now in front of the house his wife had exited. There was no question about it, this was the house.

Margha Walser rarely went out, and never at night. And they didn't have any friends on this street. Joseph knew exactly what had taken place. Stupid woman, he grumbled.

The lights were all off. No sounds could be heard. In front of the house was a garden, surrounded by a little fence. It was a nice neighborhood.

Walser walked down the alley behind the street. He could see the back of the house. There was a light on in one of the rooms, but there were hardly any sounds. Someone was alone in there, maybe getting ready for bed.

It was starting to get cold. Walser remained motionless behind the house, a few yards behind its fence.

He just watched; a few images popped into his head but quickly disappeared. He was trying not to think about anything, but he couldn't shake the image of his wife and her tiny, guilty steps as she left the house.

The only light was turned off. The house was now completely dark. He looked at his watch. He walked a little ways, gave one last look at the front door, and, finally, walked away.

2

All humane cities clean up the filthy mess that the passage of hell leaves behind: a few hearts pierced by shiny pieces of metal, damned by a material that is far from useless in war: a dense substance incompatible with life. A dead person gets mistaken for the fallen leaves of autumn, three hoarse or soft-spoken men pick up this dead lump with their fingers, so crucial to the city's hygiene; among the chestnut-colored leaves is the body, also chestnut brown, but heavy. The city is efficient. In the sky above there is a different, courageous world.

Nonetheless, there are still some remnants of happiness to be found, growing. A woman is selling flowers, a dog is sniffing around with his snout in the air, as if the birds or the clouds were giving off a strong scent. But the sky doesn't really have a scent, except after a heavy rainfall; the sky smells like water for three hours afterward, and there's no smell gentler than this on days with no rain. The city breathes. It speaks of distant harvests, and crops stream into the city from every direction: they grow on trees, then invade the domain of Mankind. Nature pays no attention to the conspiracy of machines, the frenzied ecstasy of helicopter rotors, so eager to show off their deadly capabilities.

And Mankind, as a whole, is impervious. It is a species that survives in all the holes and crevices of the earth, resisting harsh climates, powerful bombs, and even the intensity that love instills into certain bodies at certain moments; the human species keeps its neck stretched high like a clever swan and can see over every wall; meanwhile, adolescents who pretended to pay attention to the news about their country now pretend to slip and fall, with the peaceful intention of looking up the skirts of the adolescent girls who also pretend to be concerned about their country and its problems. Everything is deceptive. It's Sunday and in this city some of the grocery stores stay open on Sundays. There are still some pears that startle passersby, and the mere physical presence of a crate of apples manages to surprise people who have just seen six soldiers inflict great violence upon someone weak and trembling.

Evil is a category created by reason. It doesn't have a supernatural origin, nor does it grow from the seeds found deep within the vegetables we eat. Evil is a category that comes about instinctually, to be sure, but also by reason, by intelligence. As though it were simply another tool a mathematician's brain might employ in trying to solve a numeric equation. Deduction, induction, evil.

But as prevalent as evil is, there is something even more widespread: the universal indifference that grows out of the fact that all our bodies are separate, are violently separated from one another, even in peacetime. Each substance is incompatible with the next, and the fact that certain of our names happen to recur over and again merely conceals the obvious: no two substances can ever really share a name.

A substantial part of the city had already been conquered by this army of neutrality, which was not really an army at all: indifference. If you want to survive, put your courage in a plastic bag and wait.

All the restaurants are still open. Joseph Walser sometimes goes out with his wife on Sunday and orders lunch.

It's Sunday and the most determined couples are kissing each other. Normal relationships don't tolerate interruptions. A man with a glass of wine in his hand is enjoying himself. Old neighbors remain behind the windows that look out on the street, so they can tell who's having his way with another man's wife. Two men light a cigarette with the same match, although they each smoke their own cigarette. They exchange pleasantries. Each individual movement traces an explicit borderline between the two bodies: I am a body and I will carry out certain movements that might displease you. My movements are not responsible for your happiness.

A man who has just eaten a tangerine and is drinking wine recounts a complex anecdote in order to defend certain recent events. A number of attentive citizens listen to the careful story line of his narrative and become convinced that life will go on unchanged, if it's true that being alive today bears any connection to the fact of having been alive yesterday. The essential characteristics of life remain. And what are these characteristics? Here are a few: there's still water and air outside, and you can wiggle your toes even while appearing to remain completely motionless; it's astonishing, that you can wiggle your toes while appearing to remain completely motionless. Life has certain schizoid characteristics; the following, for instance.

Take notice: the city is still curious, indeed many citizens want to increase their nonessential knowledge while others are being gunned down in the middle of town squares that are right out in the open, not tucked away, out of sight. One of Joseph Walser's neighbors enrolled in a foreign-language school yesterday. Adult men are seated at proper school desks, meekly learning the first syllables of a language that's completely unknown to them. And it may not even be the language of the conquering army; sometimes school-learning is obscenely useless: a woman who lives on some street in the city began to learn an esoteric language, from a country with very few inhabitants and of little consequence. If you were to ask this woman why, she would say: curiosity.

Yes, the curiosity of women and men remains intact, which is almost magnificent, a thing of great value in wartime; like a vase that can't be shattered, curiosity did not break; not curiosity about essential and urgent matters, but rather curiosity about things away in the remote corners of knowledge: more than one woman yesterday enrolled in a class on the consequences of the movements of heavenly bodies. Thus, in the lives of certain people, fighter jets are nothing more than mere obstacles in their field of vision, noisy particles of dust that block their view of what's going on in the daily life of the cosmos. When you're ashamed of what you're not doing, news about events occuring close to you is taken in as if from a distance; one's entire auditory faculty becomes engaged in the techniques of cynicism, merely feigning interest. There is no formula for indifference; there are many ways to survive, and neutrality is just one of them.

Nevertheless, two lovers kiss each other once more and decide not to put off the wedding. So long as your shadow still reproduces the image of your entire body on the ground, you can rest assured that you're alive and whole.

CHAPTER V

1

Joseph Walser spent all day Sunday in his study, with the door locked, busy with his collection. A lot of Sundays were like that. The room belonged to him alone; he kept the only key.

Margha didn't even know what was in there. She had the vague notion that her husband's collection was made up of pieces of metal, but she never really understood. She didn't ask about it. She didn't dare go into her husband's study and only as a last resort would she knock on the door.

"It's my collection," Joseph Walser would say, in his crudely simple way.

She had learned to respect her husband's private domain: it was as though a highly conspicuous secret were being harbored there, as plain as day, in her own home. Joseph Walser was a capable, serious man, and it would be ridiculous for Margha to cause trouble over something that, while it was an obsession, was so harmless and inconsequential.

That room took the place of the bedroom for the children they never wanted to have; it was the nursery, or at least that's what Margha called it. Joseph spent practically all his free time there, in that room, with the door locked.

"You came home late last night," said Margha

"Yes," responded Joseph Walser, "the game went late."

2

After work on Tuesday, Joseph Walser didn't go straight home. He had asked to leave work a little early and headed resolutely to the offices that housed the records of property owners throughout the city.

He had written the street number on a piece of paper, but quickly tore it up. He didn't need it.

The house from which Joseph Walser saw his wife emerge was number 48 on Krumpfrot Street. He grabbed the list of addresses, telephone numbers, and names, and began to leaf through it. Dorlein Street, Kasch M. Street, Krumpbil Street, Krump Datsch Street, Krumpfrot Street.

Krumpfrot. There it was on the page. With the index finger of his right hand touching the page, he began to go down the page line by line, softly reading aloud the names:

26 Krumpfrot Street: Ortho Dudvik
38 Krumpfrot Street: Bother Blau
46 Krumpfrot Street: Blorghst Vrulbn
48 Krumpfrot Street: Klober Muller.

CHAPTER VI

1

The game didn't end as usual on that Saturday night at Fluzst's house. Soon after Joseph Walser left, the dice stopped rolling. The men started talking about the war; the city was essentially occupied, and had been taken with ease. They mentioned the names of some of the people who'd been killed; others had fled. At one point Fluzst said:

". . . a group that could work from here on the inside, like a network of saboteurs. Over time, little disturbances can have important consequences."

The others remained silent. The door had been shut for some time, there was no chance that Clairie, Fluzst's wife, could hear them.

"I don't want my wife to know," he had said.

There was a guilty silence between them all. Fluzst and Blukvelt were basically the only ones who spoke; the other two fellow players just listened. From time to time someone said: "This is dangerous."

Fluzst was the one most engaged by the idea.

"We don't need patience, what we really need is impatience, instigation. Planning and instigation."

2

All across the city there was already a fascination with big weapons, with domination by force. Fascination with having an important master; people just feel safer when receiving big, forceful orders than when receiving tiny, weak ones.

"We're braver when we receive forceful orders," said one of the four men. "That's true for most people."

"We no longer even control our own speech," said Fluzst. "Yesterday I was reprimanded in the middle of the street for saying a proverb. They said that type of language was inappropriate."

"There are less phrases being used in the city, which is odd, because there are more people. People are becoming as afraid of mouths willing to speak as they are of the mouths of prostitutes who look ill," someone added.

This absurd observation got a lot of laughs. They were all nervous.

The four men fell silent a number of times on this night, which never happened when they were playing. During one silent moment someone said:

"We're missing Walser."

"I don't trust him," replied Fluzst. "We're not missing anybody."

CHAPTER VII

1

He came to work on time. He shook the strong hand of his boss, Klober Muller, with his own strong hand. They looked at each other for a few seconds before Joseph lowered his eyes and looked down at their hands, still engaged in the handshake. The handshake came to an end, as is the habit among the living. Walser was clearly uncomfortable. A few weeks had passed.

"My dear Joseph," said Klober, "the gravediggers are working with different shovels, they're increasing the usual speed of their movements, and in that way increasing the average speed of their tools, an innovation proper to these none-too-slow times, my friend. There's a feeling that those big black plastic bags are heading our way, and many poets are already reading poems about them in dulcet voices—though some of them have already lost their legs. Existence itself, my dear Joseph, is ceasing to exist, which is startling, if you look at it from a certain perspective. The circle is shrinking toward its center until it is reduced to just a dot.

Walser, my friend, don't take this in the same way you might some trivial geometry lesson: everything that's about to happen will not only be recorded in History books, in their well-documented pages with large photographs; everything that's about to happen will also be inscribed upon the survivors, because there are always survivors, Walser, and it is in them, as shocking as this may seem, that death is most apparent. The dead die, it's true, nothing new there. They're buried, hidden from sight; they quickly disappear; but for the sentimental, disappearances are the most tolerable of events. Who is moved to compassion when faced with a disappearance, when faced with something that is no longer seen, when faced with the invisible? Only the insane are moved to compassion by the invisible, and you, my good sir—just like many other good citizens of this city—don't want to be thought of as insane. Insanity is a very unpleasant thing, it doesn't look good in a biography.

"But there's a disposition, my dear Joseph Walser, a disposition toward essential things for which we still don't have names. Mankind tends to move along a line toward a certain end-point, that's clear enough. You don't have to study complex geometric patterns, any old fool knows very well what it is to be afraid, what it is to be terrified, and the whole city has this disposition.

"There are some men, however, who have demonstrated an excessive imperfection: some fled to the forest and, more than just carrying firearms, they're shooting them, my dear sir. It's an absolute abomination, this shooting they're doing.

"Walser, my dear friend, I know your character and courage well, I know exactly what someone like you is capable of. Your enemies must be very afraid of you! You and many others like you are the cornerstone of this city, its center. You, my friend, will never leave here, you'll never abandon your home, at least as long as the walls remain upright and strong, protecting your head from the cold west winds; you, my good sir, will never flee to the forest.

"You're a man of good taste, Walser, it's clear in every decision you make: an interesting wife, a house that's perfectly in order, with good air circulation and smoke ventilation; maybe it even has a little garden where, every so often, when you're not feeling well, you'll disgorge the results of a mild convulsion in your stomach, brought on by too much wine. My dear Walser, as long as wine is still making its maternal way into your system, you, dear sir, won't move a muscle in defense of your homeland. Your homeland, like that of all men who are at least sensible and reasonably rational, is circumscribed by certain holidays and years of peace. To be a patriot in peacetime is to be a coward, because it's too easy! But you, Mr. Walser, don't deserve such epithets, because you're a man who inspires trust: we know exactly what you're going to do, what side you'll be on when it becomes clear which side has won. During times of confusion you retreat like any other animal with the ability to reason; your intelligence is admirable, Walser, and I know that the fact that you don't talk much is just, once again, a brilliant strategy. You'll survive, and you deserve to. You'll end up illustrating—in an impeccable manner—the principal pages of the History books to come. I see in you a certain graphical intuition, a clear perception of where best to place the pictures of bombings and speeches transcribed from television, now translated into the language of those who had the most weapons at their disposal. You, Walser, are a particular sort of thing, what might be called a versatile worker, it's in your eyes: you'll do whatever is necessary to maintain your habits. Your urine will maintain a perfectly level concentration of elements from the beginning of the war until the end. It's obvious that, on the inside, your body is made up of substances that do not change; it's startling to even imagine you growing old. Your nature is that of an astonishing eternity; you're a perfect copy of that which, in this life, is commonly called wise. When there's confusion the sensible man retreats and the brave imbecile advances, that's History, and you, my friend, are one of the main characters.

"It's true, my dear Walser, I can tell that you have anxieties, but don't bother with them, because anxieties are a drain on intelligence. I'm going to clear it all up immediately so that you don't waste your energy unnecessarily. Dear Walser, never forget that you're one of our best employees. Respect follows you wherever you go, in spite of your irresponsible shoes. But I don't want to draw this speech out too long. My dear friend, my dear Joseph Walser, yes: I'm sleeping with your wife, and if you really want to know, I'm only somewhat enthusiastic about it. But I have no doubts about you, and I hope to never have any. Joseph Walser: I'm a great admirer of yours."

CHAPTER VIII

1

Fluzst became more involved every day in activities seeking to disrupt the new human order of the city. At night he met with others; they whispered nouns, they lowered the intensity of the sound of their language, and increased the proximity of their words to facts. The words themselves did not act, but some of them did goad the body of the person speaking them so much that failing to act would become a cowardly obscenity, unacceptable for any man who wanted to be able to look at himself as though he were still a man.

They decided on locations; perhaps the city has been duplicated, and another, second city exists now at night. It's useless to be mysterious when you're the conqueror, but it's essential when you're in the position of the conquered. Only the strongest have the right to be redundant and predictable, monotony is the privilege of having attained a great height and a great clarity, the privilege of the light that is rationally distributed to everything in existence. Good illumination is a characteristic of strength; weakness plots and is so stingy with lightbulbs that this stinginess starts to become confused with its fears and its strategy. Fluzst had decreased the length of the phrases he spoke in public and had become reserved; he still hosted the dice game in his house on Saturdays, but the atmosphere had changed. There was now an aggressive judiciousness about all of them.

2

Joseph Walser is once again back in front of his machine. The work continues to move forward in a state of purity, uncontaminated by those things that are making other people suffer.

The companies in the empire of Leo Vast, who owns the factory, move on apace. The world is variegated, even within a single geographic space. A few square yards of earth can cover multiple corpses, stacked on top of each other, or they can bring forth the promise of a garden. Within a single city there are hundreds of cities; the mere fact of being a man isn't enough to be able to found your own city, but it's almost enough.

It's like this: each survivor and each individual fear founds a hypothetical city, a metropolis, which is transitory and fragile, to be sure, but all metropolises are.

Joseph Walser is taking a little break right now, stepping away from his piping-hot machine, which is almost suffocating him after two straight hours of exertion. These pauses are becoming more and more important, because the excessive heat from the machine and his own fatigue get intermingled with the noise from the sirens that flood in through the windows during the brief silences of the motor, which is located just inches away from Walser's chest.

Joseph Walser is getting older, but he still reveres "his" machine and all its inner workings. At various moments the sound of the motor and its vibrations get interwoven with the beating of his heart as well, for both of these "organs" are functioning perfectly, in a state of perfect excitation; they are pressed up against each other and thus start to become intermingled, which causes ridiculous jolts of alarm in Walser, from time to time, when, at precisely planned moments, the machine's motor suddenly stops. It is at those times that Walser notices the connection between his body and the machine. These sudden stops cause an instantaneous, cold shiver to cascade over his skin: a brief sensation, and one so unpleasant that it prompts him, for example, to look through scientific textbooks to find a detailed description of what a person feels when his heart fails. Walser tries to figure out if the brutal division of the functioning of his heart from the functioning of the machine's motor, whenever it stops, is anything like the division of a man's heart from the man himself. He has read that a non-fatal heart attack is sometimes described in this way: *the organ retreats from us, at great speed . . . but then it comes back.*

The heart retreats from the rest of the body. Retreat, that is the essential word. A distance is traveled during a heart attack, a distance that is traveled internally: one of the organs marches in a direction opposite from the rest of the body. And that was what Walser felt when he was stimulated and engulfed in the operation of his machine, and the machine suddenly stopped; and it didn't just stop for some unknown reason, some reason that would require inductive reasoning in order to comprehend, it simply stopped because it was twelve o'clock, and at twelve o'clock all the machines' motors were switched off at the factory's central offices.

Walser wasn't going to die, this became apparent to him one second after each stoppage, but the immediate sensation, throughout his entire organism, irrational and inexplicable, was one of sadness. You could almost say that Walser's entire organism became melancholic the moment that the machine's motor stopped and he became conscious that, ultimately, there were two separate things at work there: himself and the machine. Two incompatible, separable things, two things that could retreat from each other. Yes, his melancholy derived from this obvious fact: he and the machine were two separate things that could retreat from each other. When the motor stopped Walser saw himself fully exposed in the world; he looked all around: everything could retreat from everything else.

During these breaks Walser sometimes did something that, if he were to be observed from start to finish, might lead people to classify him as insane: he would walk over to one of the work tables, which were set up against a wall, and pull on it, as if he wanted to measure the force necessary to separate one object from another, and, at the same time, to feel how easy it was to do it. The table was made of a hardwood, it was a heavy, compact table, with a number of tools on top; and Walser, instead of using the time while the motor was stopped to rest, and without any planning beforehand, instinctively walked over to the table and then strenuously pulled it away from the wall. He had been reprimanded many times for this useless and slightly irritating act, but it was clear that a table being pulled a few inches away from the wall wasn't going to cause the ruin of the factory. It's just that the act of pulling the table was absolutely unnecessary.

"My dear Walser," Klober Muller always told him, "how many times have I told you that the table needs to remain against the wall? Do you hear me, my good sir?"

Joseph Walser's expression of perfect concentration irritated Klober and the other workers, but at the same time it was clear that the act of pulling the table didn't constitute an affront. It was unthinkable that Walser could commit an affront. This tiny disturbance, repeated many times over, was, for all that, completely undervalued by the managers of the factory, who considered it the natural product of a strange but basically sensible personality. Seen from the outside, the act of pulling the table was just a quirk.

On that day, Joseph Walser went back to his post after another short break at three o'clock, pressing his body against his machine to once again initiate the necessary movements. The motor began to run, as scheduled, at three ten. Walser's chest rested vertically along a piece of metal that was slightly uncomfortable at its lower extremity, which was level with his stomach; each of his feet was in place on the appropriate pedal and began to fall into the rhythm that they would maintain, as usual, for an entire hour; his hands were already in their proper positions inside the machine and fit precisely into their little slots, which only allowed for the movements that were necessary for the operation of the machine. Yet Walser felt that the shirtsleeve on his left arm was caught, so started to move his other hand, letting go of its lever for a few seconds in order to resolve this unforeseen situation. Suddenly, his left hand slipped out from its place in the machine, and, quite distinct from the other noises in the factory, a colossal scream emerged from the mouth of the employee Joseph Walser.

PART II

CHAPTER IX

1

Lying on the hospital bed, Joseph Walser watched the patient who, for the last few minutes, hadn't stopped laughing. The man, a fat man, could barely move on top of his bed, and his chest shook with each peal of laughter. A nurse asked him to calm down.

Out in the hallway, incoherent sounds would at times come together to form a cluster that was intelligible, and in these moments there was a feeling that there was going to be an attack on the hospital. The sounds, however, quickly undid their structural unity, or so it seemed, and the shapeless incoherence returned, demonstrating that nothing had changed. Men emitting weak sounds were held up by men emitting voices that were still virile and healthy. The vibration of all the sounds and the way in which the words either resounded or fell flat allowed Walser to distinguish between health and illness, since he couldn't manage to see anyone from his room, except for his fat roommate who finally stopped making such a racket.

Inside Walser's body, his sensibility to sounds seemed to be turned up to maximum intensity, as if controlled by a switch. Any defects in the space in which he lay were consequences of the defects in the sounds surrounding him; if the sounds from the hallway and the other rooms bothered him, the quality of the whole environment seemed to deteriorate.

Short sounds were emitted by energetic nurses and doctors. An odd relationship had already become obvious: those who acted spoke very little, and when they did use words, they sounded ruthless, almost malicious. But the ones who gave the appearance of being unaffected by the suffering that could be heard all around were the ones who turned out to be the most useful: grabbing a pair of scissors, cutting bandages that had become uncomfortable, making quick notes in their notebooks, adjusting the position of the beds at the patients' request, administering medication.

All of a sudden the central mass of sounds changed. A tremendous commotion seemed to be arising out of some similarly gigantic indecision about what movements should be made. Nurses and doctors raised their voices. All this foretold the arrival of something, and one or another person ran through the hallway, which marked a clear change in behavior. From the open door of his room, Walser could see the first stretcher pass by at great speed, a stretcher bearing a body with a significant wound. His first impulse was to raise his torso up off his bed so he would be in a better position to see. But he could still only see very little.

The sounds continued, and Walser had the strange feeling that his eyes, at that moment, were jealous of his ears, since there was such an enormous amount of material for his ears to interpret. He was on the verge, absurd as it was, of yelling: "I want to see!" But he didn't say anything, out of shyness.

The sound of accelerated footsteps on the floor became essential. Walser immediately thought of his brown shoes, his irresponsible shoes, as his boss Klober had put it. The sound that he now heard from the hallways, however, couldn't be from irresponsible shoes. "Something's happened," he murmured. There was great gravity in the sound of those fast-moving shoes.

Meanwhile, his roommate was also trying to discern what was going on. His completely uncontrolled and unjustified bursts of laughter had come to such a natural end that Walser hadn't even noticed the difference. It was clear that something important was happening. More stretchers had passed by, and Walser had seen a number of uniformed bodies lying on them. Certain sounds stuck out as having been individual words amid all the tumult, in which other sounds seemed both neutral and unintelligible; these words took on a personality, as if, paradoxically, they were the only sounds weighty enough to remain afloat in the air after all the others had disappeared: "attack" and "bomb" could now be heard clearly.

2

The exteriors of prominent buildings had been modified; a building can always be dated with reference to important moments in time: for instance, before and after the explosion.

The explosion emerged from that hazy borderline between the elements and etched itself onto the human physiognomy in a strange and immediate way.

The attack occurred in the late afternoon, near a military outpost. The windows of a house—possibly tempered by the lack of curiosity of its owners—survived the impact intact. Two quiet old men who were in the vicinity remained silent. Only momentous changes, be they negative or positive, can modify ancient substances, which is precisely what certain old men are. An elderly couple woke up: "An explosion," someone said.

Meanwhile the deft fire was making its way along the path of whatever materials burned best. Pieces of wood that burn quickly fell to the ground in minutes. The thigh of an adorable woman was inflicted with a shallow cut, which, surrounded by her prominent beauty, seemed obscene and inappropriate. Even so, death is disorderly; it doesn't just descend upon the ugly and useless.

Soldiers who, from a distance, look more like the embodiment of History than people with real human characteristics, soon become enemies of this sort of abstract thinking once they get up close—because they can bleed. Once an evil as aggressive and impatient as a bomb gets too close to unprepared human bodies, it penetrates them, each piece of shrapnel entering like an unwanted morsel of food—death becoming defined as a wide fissure in the human body.

The attack was an attempt on the life of Ortho, the most important leader of the band of troops occupying the city, but it didn't succeed. He was wounded, and was now dealing with the immediate damage and helping to attend to the dead soldiers who, a second earlier—back when they were still alive—had been accompanying him.

Two men were seen rapidly fleeing the scene. Ortho gave orders to search the area immediately: whoever detonated the bomb was close by, trying to get away.

And so the search for the two men moves forward, in the opposite direction of the ambulances that are just now arriving on the scene; the sound of the wind is so quiet and the clouds are so high and neutral that the ambulance sirens seem to be the only things in existence at this moment; only human elements are allowed to participate in certain specific activities epitomizing human intelligence—which is what a well-planned act of retaliation is, after all.

It's true that unhappiness isn't solely contingent on the presence of pain, but happiness, on the other hand, should be solely contingent on the absence of physical pain. Twenty centuries, whole and complete, haven't been able to produce an explanation of suffering; suffering only exists by contrast with not suffering, and healthy men don't want to be told about anything bad before it actually occurs. Resistance to pain must be practiced: people avoid any contact with that repulsive "thing."

Certain soldiers called their shrapnel wounds "inverted caresses," as if these reminded them of the display of infantile, childhood emotions. The world is constantly being traversed by both honest and dishonest angels; at times it even seems that buildings themselves are mobile, urban beings that have concrete wills all their own. A building collapsed.

The music on the radio is interrupted, and the microphone is handed over to a soldier who talks about an unfortunate incident and the righteous military force that is preparing to respond to it.

The curiosity of the masses comes in remarkable waves of repugnance and perversion; a tall man stands on his tiptoes and pushes a tiny woman because he wants to be the first to be sad, as if his number had been the first one called at the county recorder's office; he stretches out his legs, which are already long, and sees bodies that are less logical, blacker, and more spread out from one another than they normally are, and picks up a certain frightening odor. Catastrophes pave the way for the appearance of benevolent Princes, who are equipped to reinstate civilization. Colossal kindness requires the necessary spectators; a man comes through the crowd yelling certain things, saying that he's a doctor. The crowd gives him room, and the man who is a doctor passes through, proud that he has learned the secret names of medications and the precise ways to grip certain tools for the good of the city. Speed; cars honk their horns, the flow of vehicles seeks out the route that best suits the dead, the sky reduces its number of birds, which have either made themselves scarce or seem to be intruding impolitely: nobody can allow other songs to be sung when the national anthem has to be played, or when people are going to think it to themselves, even when these songs are coming from serene birds, who are in any case accustomed to being discreet and stepping aside whenever humans decide to exchange strong words or gunfire.

And the search continues: two men had been seen, but no one got a good look at them. There are some worthless clues, weak leads. Someone who said something, someone who saw something or almost saw something, someone who's full of hunches and points around with his index finger a lot. Soldiers go into the houses that are near the site of the explosion, ask questions, respond brusquely to insignificant answers, but there's no other kind of answer to be had; they make great haste, there's a certain nervous excitement in the people, the enemy is sought with an inexplicable enthusiasm, love has never been sought after like this, never at any time, never in any place has anyone ever been so passionate in love as they now are in hatred; short-haired soldiers ask about family members who aren't present, long explanations are given, one's personal world finally begins to make sense when one is afraid, when one's fear is great.

And thus it so happened that two men crossed paths in a neighborhood not too far away, walking in opposite directions; and their speed was suddenly curtailed. The two men stopped and looked; one is the boss of the other.

"Fluzst?"

"Foreman Klober."

"Fluzst, in this part of town? Who would've guessed it? Did you hear the explosion? Have you heard what happened? Just look how you're shaking, Fluzst, and look at your face! Are you scared? And that smell. How very interesting to find you here!"

CHAPTER X

1

A few hours had passed since the uproar. Sounds had returned back to normal, as well as movements. Apparently whatever had happened was no longer happening. The effects of whatever had happened had receded far away, to some other part of the hospital. As if they'd been forgotten about, thinks Walser.

And it was clear, at that moment, that memory must be intimately connected to space. Memory is a characteristic of space, not of people. A simple characteristic, like height, length, and width. "Memory is the fourth immediate characteristic of space," says Walser to himself, as if about to make some important discovery. But sounds are also a characteristic of space, and there in the hospital room, still the most significant.

Walser is sitting with his legs stretched out along the length of the bed and his torso upright. He is trying to spot a nurse, but he can't see anyone. He calls out for one in a loud voice.

The incidental background noises are still present. The situation is calm, but Walser wants to get out of there. He again calls out for a nurse or a doctor. No one comes. The murmuring sound of a quiet conversation can be heard somewhere in the hallway. They're close by, it isn't possible that nobody can hear Walser's calls.

Joseph Walser is starting to get nervous: he'd had an accident, a significant accident, they have to pay attention to him, but the sounds of the nurses aren't close enough for the attention he requires. He, Joseph Walser, had a serious accident, at work, with his machine; they should respect that.

"They don't hear anybody," says his roommate.

"I've spent hours calling out to them," the roommate says later, and then abruptly bursts into laughter.

"Hours!" he repeats.

Walser screamed as loud as he could. Then stopped. He remembered the scream he let out at the moment the accident occurred. This more recent scream was similar, with just one difference: it was planned, thought out in advance, a strategic scream, as opposed to the other one; it was a false scream, he realized. I'm not in any pain: that was a false scream.

But Walser didn't feel uneasy about this momentary falsehood; the fact that he realized what he was doing didn't stop him from repeating the action. He screamed again, as loud as he could, as if he were in need of urgent care.

He grew more annoyed by the minute. His roommate's outburst of laughter had stopped, but, despite Walser's clamoring, there was no change in the background noise out in the hallways.

He stood up, swung his legs over the edge of the bed, and, with his left hand on the bed for support, stepped down onto the floor.

He was barefoot and was hiding his right hand behind his back. The feeling of the cold floor under his feet hit him with a concrete, sensual violence, which he was almost relieved to feel: he was tired of feeling the world through sound alone.

The shiver that shot up from his feet soon subsided. The human organism is an absolutely flawless machine that reacts immediately: intelligent enough to sense changes in temperature.

He took a cautious step first, then another one, and his feet heated up the cold floor beneath them, or vice versa. At least I'm not wearing irresponsible shoes, thought Walser, almost cracking a smile.

He was now at the doorway to the room. He walked forward a little bit more and saw, about thirty feet away, two nurses and a doctor. This time he called out to them with much more self-control, almost embarrassed: "Nurse!"

But it was the doctor who walked over to him.

2

Klober the foreman looked Fluzst over from head to toe, and a wide grin appeared on his face, which was soon cut short by a return to seriousness.

"Looks like the city was entitled to one more attack," said Klober.

Fluzst nodded in assent, and Klober went on in the same ironic tone with which he had begun:

"This only proves that we are an important city. A city! No one would ever think about planting a bomb in the countryside, in the middle of a bunch of pigs," he said laughing.

"This is proof of the advent of civilization: we have libraries and bomb attacks. But our bombs aren't arriving as neat packages delivered by the army; disorder has affected even our weapons and has spread to the crudest and least intellectually capable segment of the population; and thus the danger grows. Disorder and weaponry aren't compatible, in my humble opinion, and killing isn't purely an action, it also requires some intellectual ability. But what have you got to say about all this, Fluzst, you've got a frightened look on your face, you've just come from the area where the bomb went off . . .

"You probably didn't see anything, is that right? That's what I thought. We're all blind. A city full of blind people. But we've still got good ears, perfectly effective auricular devices. In other words, some parts of the city are still functioning. My dear Fluzst, I must bid you good-bye. I want to see what happened up close. I, too, have the right to be frightened. It's odd seeing you like this, on such an important day. You are one of our liveliest workers, don't go losing all that energy now, we're counting on you. All right, I'll see you tomorrow, won't I?

"Oh, I forgot to tell you something. An important piece of information: your coworker Joseph Walser had an accident with his machine. He's in the hospital. I know you two are good friends. He would certainly appreciate a visit from you. Have a good one, Fluzst—and pull yourself together. We're counting on you."

3

"Doctor," said Walser, still hiding his right arm against the side of his body, "I'm sorry, but I've been calling for a nurse for quite some time."

The doctor didn't respond. He looked steadily at Walser.

"What's your name?"

"Joseph Walser."

"Joseph Walser," repeated the doctor. "Well then, Mr. Walser, please behave yourself. You're in a hospital!" said the doctor, turning his back on him.

A nurse came over to him.

"This isn't a time for weakness, my dear sir. What happened to you is child's play. You'd be doing a big favor to all of us if you would just behave like a man."

Joseph muttered something and felt his face turn ruby-red.

"Go back to your bed," said the nurse, "when someone becomes available they'll attend to you and get your papers in order so you can leave. Please go back to your room."

4

Fluzst entered his house in a hurry and immediately locked the door, turning the lock three times. His wife, Clairie, ran over to him.

"What happened?"

Fluzst didn't respond and headed toward the bathroom.

"Bring me alcohol and make these clothes disappear."

He took off his clothes.

"Everything's fine. I'm going to take a bath. Pick up all these clothes and burn them."

"Are you hurt?"

"Don't be stupid. Do as I say."

CHAPTER XI

1

With his wife at his side, Joseph Walser walked into his house. His gestures were cautious, succinct, and completely restricted to his left hand. He kept his right arm at his side, no matter what position his body happened to be in, and he held his right hand, shamefully, behind his back.

Even though he'd only been away for a day, that absence made it so that he entered this familiar space as though he had suddenly recovered a lost memory. He looked at the desk where he kept the key to his study.

"Do you want to be alone?" asked Margha.

Joseph Walser didn't respond. He walked straight over to the key, grabbed it with his left hand, and used the same hand to open the door. In the meantime, his wife backed away from him.

Joseph Walser stepped into his study; the customary noise of the lock as it was locked from the inside. Margha sat down; she cried.

Joseph Walser stood before his collection. He felt comforted: everything in its place. Countless pieces of metal were arranged in an orderly fashion on over fifty shelves. And below each one was a label with a corresponding number. On the desk, directly across the room from the door, there was a notebook with a black cover, and beside it a gray, shiny ruler.

Walser had started his collection eight years earlier. He picked up any piece of metal he could find, but with two restrictions: they had to be solitary pieces, not connected to anything else—thus, unattached to any other components; and each of the dimensions of the piece—length, height, and width—had to measure less than four inches.

The sight of his perfectly organized collection was oddly comforting to him, given that it had only been one day since his accident. He smiled: with his left hand he searched around in his coat pocket for the metal object he had brought home from the hospital. It was the round wheel guard from one of the stretchers. It had come loose and fallen on the floor, and Walser had snatched it up.

Over the years he had developed an exceptional perceptive ability when it came to pieces of metal that could possibly have a place in his collection. His perception of reality and events gradually transformed into a dual perception: he watched events as they took place and eventually ended, and sometimes he even took part in these events as they happened—which constituted his lived experience—but behind this level of perception, which sought out the best means of survival, Walser had a second level of perception, or perhaps the same level of perception, but with a second set of objectives, which, instead of being focused on people and their interactions, or on the things that could interfere with these interactions, was focused on his search for small metal objects.

He was perfectly aware that his collection was, beyond being merely useless, absurd. He never talked about it. Even in his own house, as we've stated, he was the only one with a key to the study, where he organized his "finds." It was clear that his wife, Margha, had seen some of these pieces of metal, but she was forbidden to enter the room, and Joseph had never spoken to her about it. The only references he ever made to it were by way of these simple, almost abstract, words: "my collection."

Joseph Walser pulled out the chair and sat down. He rested his left hand on the desk. Everybody already knew what had happened during the accident.

For the first time since the day before, he paid exclusive attention to his right hand: he started to raise his arm, a movement that seemed obscene to him at first. But he didn't stop.

He slowly laid his right hand on the desk next to his left hand. He looked directly at his hand, which was still closed into a fist, and then opened his hand, spreading apart his fingers. He focused all his attention on his right hand. There were only four fingers resting on the desktop. They had amputated his index finger.

2

"You should go visit him. They had to amputate one of his fingers."

Fluzst was still uneasy, but his wife insisted on telling him about what had happened at the factory: Walser's accident.

"His hand slipped, no one really knows how it happened. His sleeve got caught on one of the levers of the machine. He's already back from the hospital, he's back at home; you should go visit him tonight. You're his friend."

Fluzst was smoking a cigarette. He was trying to calm himself down.

"Joseph Walser is a coward," he said. "He won't miss that finger at all."

3

He had opened the anatomy textbook to the chapter entitled "Hand."

There was one drawing after another of hands in different positions, each one with five fingers.

Joseph Walser looked at the names for the first time. Names of things that had belonged to him for quite some time. The "*opponens pollicis* (thumb muscle)," the "*flexor retinaculum* of the hand," the "adductor," the "abductor."

The skeleton of the hand made a real impression on him. In the wrist area, eight little bones were stacked on top of each other: "carpal bones," he read. Then, between the wrist and the fingers, the five metacarpal bones, one for each finger. Each of the fingers, in turn, was made of three consecutive bones, "like train cars," he muttered; their names were almost infantile: "proximal phalanges, intermediate phalanges, distal phalanges." The thumb was an exception in this case: it only had two phalanges, instead of the three phalanges the other fingers had.

It was simple: the amputation of his index finger, in concrete and objective terms, had removed three phalanges from his body. Of the fourteen phalanges that he used to have on his right hand, now only eleven remained. On his left hand he still had the fourteen phalanges he was born with.

He looked at the drawings of the muscles of the hand. The two essential movements of the fingers: flexion and extension. Each finger had a flexor muscle that was attached to the distal phalange. He would never again be able to flex or extend the index finger on his right hand.

Muscles and bones were the two essential substances that Walser had lost in the accident. All the other substances were basically supports for these two, which were responsible for two movements, flexion and extension. With the anatomy textbook open, Joseph Walser once again set his hands on the desk and opened them wide. He looked at the drawings: ten fingers. He looked at his hands: nine fingers.

He suddenly became terrified, as if he were looking at the hands of a monster.

CHAPTER XII

1

With his left hand, Walser took the metal object that he'd brought home from the hospital out of his pocket and placed it on the desktop. With some of the fingers of his right hand he opened his notebook and began to turn the pages until he reached the one he was looking for.

His right hand was perfectly functional. His eyes still seemed astonished by the empty space where his index finger had been, but his hand, apparently, continued to behave like a group that had decided, internally, to continue to carry out its mission regardless. Immediately after the first few movements of his hand, it seemed clear to Walser that his index finger hasn't been indispensable. Without thinking about it for a single second, so that he didn't start to feel apprehensive about it, he grabbed a ruler with his right hand, placing it alongside the piece of metal he held with his left. All these things were resting on top of the desk: the piece of metal, his left hand, his right hand, and the ruler. He looked down at these four objects as though they were four elements, four elements that were completely separated from one another, yet belonged to the same family: the family of "things." What other words could be used to describe them? Visible things, four visible things?

Ever since he first saw the absurd empty space where his index finger used to be, he realized that his fingers were just things, like any other thing; his whole hand was a thing, like anything else, a thing that could be separated from him, exactly like the ruler and the piece of metal.

With the three fingers of his right hand supported by his thumb, Walser slid the ruler up against the piece of metal and measured its length: 3.6 inches. He'd guessed right once again. It was a piece that could be part of his collection: the longest of its dimensions was still under four inches.

Yes, it was impressive to see how well Walser's eyes had been trained when it came to such minute measurements. He rarely picked up an object that surpassed the required maximum and would thus have to be excluded from his collection. It was as though his eyes had, over the years, acquired a new feature, a feature stolen from this most practical and functional tool: the ruler. As such, it wasn't long before Walser had progressed to the point where he began ascribing certain affective qualities to concrete measurements. Emotionally—and this was all to do with emotions, sometimes even feelings of fright, dread, anxiety—emotionally, for Walser, the experience of seeing, in space, wherever that space happened to be, a piece of metal longer than four inches was completely different from the experience of seeing one that was shorter than four inches. His constant use of the ruler, which from the very first had been an affective tool for him (Walser had abandoned the idea that the ruler functioned in the service of scientific objectivity early on), eventually transformed his very nature, this "metrical affectivity" being transferred from the ruler to Walser's own perceptive capacity. Thus, it might be said that the very dimensions of a given piece of metal were capable of directly influencing Walser's feelings of excitement or disappointment.

His collection had become such an obsession that the moment Walser saw a piece of metal that met the required conditions, his concentration on it became unwavering; this intense concentration could be called predatory (predatory concentration, a hunter's concentration). It was unwavering until the moment came when nobody was paying attention, which allowed Walser to grab the piece—or, rather, to steal it (this verb could certainly be used to describe the act, since that was precisely what Walser was doing).

Many—though not all—of the times someone was compelled to ask that familiar question ("Are you listening, Mr. Walser?") he was, Walser, instead of paying attention to his interlocutor, or indeed the concrete external experience that he was sharing with this particular person at this particular time, attuned to some piece of metal and, consequently, the actions that would be necessary to obtain it. His continual lack of awareness during conversations and his often quirky behavior both certainly resulted from the same cause: his collection. Useless, absurd, and secret, it had gradually become the center of Walser's existence. He enjoyed his wife's company, even after it became clear that she was sleeping with Klober Muller, the foreman; he also took a certain, inexplicable physical pleasure in working at his machine, and he still liked to join his friends in the dice game they played for money, but his collection constituted the one real individual mark that Joseph Walser felt he would leave on the world. A unique mark, one that couldn't be copied; no one else had a collection like his.

It was an "irrational" collection, more irrational than the usual sorts of collection already are, and this fact set Walser apart from other men. Joseph Walser had been educated to function with absolute rationality, to participate in the mandatory, continual evaporation of unreason that is always interfering with the lives of men. He knew very well that it was Reason that protected him, that allowed him to defend himself, even more so now that the chaos of the war, the military occupation, and the bomb attacks were becoming, more and more each day, a source of increasing and widespread danger: nothing at all was beyond the reach of the disorder that had descended upon the city.

Nevertheless, Walser had never been as obsessive about his collection as he'd grown in the last few months. The more the disorder and unpredictability of the war grew, the more time Walser spent locked away in his study taking measurements: width, length, and height, drawing the shape of a piece of metal as well as the machine or simple structure to which it belonged, jotting down its color and function—any possible concrete functions it might have had—jotting down the place where he'd found this "precious" piece of metal, and the date and time; even compiling statistics about which spots had yielded the most specimens for his collection and the days of the week that were most providential; consulting his notebook and correcting any tiny errors from the days before, grouping the objects according to different characteristics: pieces from industrial machines, pieces from domestic or personal appliances, etc., etc.

All the specimens in his collection were thus catalogued in great detail, and their measurements recorded in his black notebook—with the roman numeral XXVI on the cover—long before the pieces of metal were placed on their respective shelves, organized according to their essential functions. This world which, when viewed from the outside, might seem illogical and strange, was in fact thoroughly ordered; it was a secondary order, one that only Walser could perceive.

Thus, what Walser did on that day wasn't at all out of the ordinary: after he put the new piece on top of his desk, his first act was to write down its measurements. After a slight hesitation, Walser slid the ruler up against the piece of metal with his right hand. He had never noticed it before, but he usually, out of instinct, laid his right index finger along the length of the ruler to hold it in place. Now, as he repeated the same movement, the fact that his index finger wasn't in the right place became obvious. Concentrating intently, he was able to stop looking at the empty place that was left by the amputated finger and focused his eyes on his middle finger, the longest finger on his hand, which slid the ruler into place in the exact same way as his index finger once did, only now he had to slightly raise the part of the palm of his hand that led up to the empty space left by the amputatation. But his middle finger was able to perform the task that his index finger had: it slid the ruler into place and kept it straight while his other hand held the piece of metal.

He had finished measuring the piece of metal that he'd stolen from the hospital. Given that it was the first time, since the accident, that he'd taken measurements, he was satisfied: he accomplished the task relatively effectively. Holding a pen in his hand, with three fingers pushing on one side and his thumb pushing on the other, Joseph Walser—albeit with hesitant, unsteady handwriting— wrote the following under the column marked height: .5.

The world is so simple, he thought.

CHAPTER XIII

1

The city calmed down in under a week. No one had been arrested in connection with the bombing, but investigations were still underway. Around the city it was said that at any moment "the culprits will be arrested" and subsequently put before the firing squad.

Joseph Walser had returned to work. Unfortunately, given the result of the accident, he couldn't return to his old post. The amputation of the index finger on his right hand eliminated any possibility of safely operating the machine that he had worked with for years. As such, it wasn't a question of psychology; Walser would have liked to go back to his machine, but a solid, concrete thing stood in his way: a simple missing finger. He didn't press the issue overmuch. Klober had said, "My dear Walser, if you had an accident while you still had five fingers on your right hand, how can you possibly want to keep working with the same machine now?"

Klober's observation wasn't just an expression of his indifference toward what had happened, it was chiefly the effect of a calculating mind that never rested, a rationality that seemed like it was never allowed a break. *The only way we can be permanently rational is by forcing our emotions to remain steady in any and all situations.*

"Like the oil inside a machine," joked Klober, "which has to remain within certain defined areas in order to be effective!"

And then, "Four fingers on your right hand aren't enough to tame this beast," said Klober to Joseph on the day he returned to work.

Walser accepted these statements without animosity; Klober's observation was sensible: the machine was difficult to operate, and in his condition he wasn't fit for the task.

He was transferred to another part of the factory, to a building that didn't have any machines. He was no longer involved in the direct production of materials and took over the duties of a clerk.

In less than three weeks he attained the ability to write smoothly without his index finger. He felt encouraged by this quick and easy progress.

Only once after the accident had he returned to the building where he used to work, to watch "his machine" in motion, now operated by some other man. At that moment, Walser felt something inside him that one could objectively call jealously, but apparently not the usual, irrational variety of this form of affect. No, the jealousy that Walser felt was a jealousy of efficiency, a rational jealousy.

At first it was a feeling of guilt. He was the one who had abandoned the machine; or, to put it another way: he was the one who had failed, and he was no longer capable of performing the necessary movements. He had betrayed the machine by losing a finger.

Of course, Walser's sadness too wasn't the same sensation as is referred to under ordinary circumstances, when we employ that word: shedding a tear in this situation would have been absurd.

Walser's sadness was—we are obliged to repeat—logical and rational; it was something that we might describe as: melancholy filtered through the sensibility of competence. Walser had the lingering sensation that he'd been expelled from an entire world, the world of machines, and that his presence would no longer be tolerated. Having lost a finger, he had also lost the abilities that commanded respect in this other universe.

Like a member of a completely different species, Walser did something on that day that he never dared to do again: when the machine was resting, with its motor turned off, he walked over to it and, with his right hand, the hand that was now deformed and reduced in size, he touched the side of the machine, touched its metal lightly, and as he touched it he felt, strangely, something like the reconstitution of the finger that had been amputated—and he smiled.

"It's still hot," he said.

CHAPTER XIV

1

The five men were seated around the table, and Fluzst had just rolled. It was Joseph Walser's turn.

Walser again grabbed the dice. He started to shake them in his hand.

"You look ridiculous rolling the dice with your left hand."

Joseph Walser raised his eyes to his colleague. Stumm was one of the new additions to the group, which had continued to meet at Fluzst's house. He had started working at the factory less than a year ago.

"It's no surprise that your wife's sleeping with another man," said Stumm, something nobody expected to hear.

The room became silent. Joseph Walser stared at his colleague for a few moments, while all the other men kept quiet. However, he then lowered his eyes and switched the dice over to his right hand.

"There you go!" said Fluzst.

Normaas, one of the other players, muttered, "Let's just play. We came here to play."

Normaas was the peacemaker of the group. He smoked constantly.

"You can't take this stuff too seriously. We're all just here to make some money," he said, letting loose a short chuckle.

The atmosphere in the room improved after this intervention. The men waited for Walser to roll.

His right hand was shaking, everyone was looking at him; and, obscenely, Stumm wouldn't take his eyes off of Walser's fingers.

"That hand of yours will bring you luck yet," he said.

Fluzst brusquely told Stumm to shut up.

"Let's play," said Fluzst, "we're all tired of waiting. Walser, please roll the dice."

2

All interruptions were prohibited. Nobody, not a single person on the entire continent had permission to rest; there was no place to hide from existence; a true, restful break has yet to be invented.

Three months had passed since the day Joseph Walser had his accident; the same day as the bombing. Having overcome their obstacles, these two lives—Walser's and the city's—had returned to their usual routines, so much so that what had happened to them no longer seemed important. Joseph Walser merely missed "his" machine. It was the absence of daily contact with its mechanisms that reminded him of the fact that he'd undergone an amputation. It was as though these two losses were two equivalent substances: the absence of his machine was the absence of his finger.

The Saturday night dice games continued, and it could be said, objectively, that Joseph Walser's luck changed for the better after his accident. He wasn't, however, winning big pots: he'd return home each Saturday night with a little more money than he'd had

when he left, but the quantities were paltry; there was no notice-
able change in the family budget. Along these lines, however, the
following should be noted: two months after his accident, the
people at the factory had taken away the hazard pay that he used
to receive for working with the machine. Since he was now doing
clerical work, it would be ridiculous to keep giving him "hazard
pay." "Writing isn't hazardous," someone had said. Thus, objectively, even after receiving compensation for his accident, Walser
made less money now. And his slight change of luck in the dice
game didn't make up the difference.

3

With the dice in his right hand, Walser held his breath. Nothing substantial was at stake in these movements, but this only became obvious after the dice were rolled and their effects became visible; effects that were significant at that moment, to be sure, but not very relevant over a longer span of time: they were insignificant from the vantage point of a week of Walser's life, and almost nonexistent when one considered an entire year. Nonetheless, at the moment before the dice were released back into the exterior world, when they were still in Walser's hand, at the moment when everything was still possible—within the limits, of course, of the dots that were inscribed on each side—at that moment, at that very second, each roll of the dice seemed as if it were able to attain a decisive density in Walser's existence. An instant before the dice left his hand, there was the feeling that "everything can change." But the dice flew from his hand and nothing changed concretely, and after the momentary jubilation or disappointment relative to whatever sides of the dice were facing upward, "nothing's changed" was what Walser's thoughts would have read, if they had suddenly become visible.

Yet, although it wasn't very significant, the change in luck that had taken place over the last little while was a source of comfort for Walser. Winning, even trifling quantities, was important: a feeling of pride—moderate, to be sure—came over him every time he gathered his winnings from the middle of the table, with his two hands: his left hand whole, compact, strong; his right hand deformed, missing its index finger, instinctively closed in upon itself, as if to protect itself from the stares of the other players—both hands, parallel to each other, pulling the money toward him from the middle of the table with a greediness that was made grotesque by the conspicuous absence of his index finger.

During the first few moments when Joseph, having been challenged by Stumm, was forced to shake the dice in his right hand, the sensation was profoundly unpleasant. The movements that he had performed with five fingers countless times before, those slight movements that had made the dice rattle in his hand, were now limited, and Joseph felt—at the precise moment when the dice rolled toward the place that his index finger used to occupy and thus couldn't complete their journey, instead having to draw back toward the palm of the hand, rolling straight from the thumb to the middle finger and then from the middle finger to the pinky—at that moment, Walser felt that someone, or something, had not only stolen a part of his body, but his movements as well. And this realization completely changed Walser's understanding of his accident: more than just a material and objective part of him—which is how Walser viewed his finger, and how he had always viewed his body parts—he had been robbed of possibilities of movement; in a word: desires. He now had intentions that he could no longer carry out.

More important than the amputation of an organic, concrete body part was the feeling that he had been defrauded of something that had been housed in his brain, yes, precisely that: something in that intimate, hidden organ, that most personal of human organs. Something of great importance had taken place in the less visible parts of his body: external reality had interfered with that which he had assumed was most protected, and which he most considered his; thus: "the furthest removed from the day-to-day." The things in his body that he had always considered "the furthest removed from the day-to-day," to take up this felicitous expression, were, without a doubt, his thoughts, his inner life—made up of his mental images, his plans, his intentions. The external world had tampered with the part of his body that he had always considered invisible, and thus untouchable.

Soon enough, with the two dice in his right hand, at the moment when the dice, instead of rolling from his middle finger to the index finger, were forced to proceed directly from his middle finger to his thumb: at that very moment, an instinctive moment—after having played many dice games under his "new material conditions" (an expression that Walser himself employed, out loud, when referring to himself)—at that essential moment, Walser no longer felt the impulse or desire to roll the dice toward the spot where his index finger had once been; that is to say: in just a few weeks' time the most violent amputation of all had been accomplished: the amputation of his desire. His immaterial being had suffered an accident, just as though it had returned to the moment of the concrete, real accident. There was no exact date for this second accident, as there was for his accident with the machine, but about three months after the first, objective date, the one that could be pointed to on a calendar, Walser lost something else.

Yet it was still strange for him to notice that, with even less possibilities available to him—with the shorter path that the dice now had to take as they rolled around in his right hand—his luck had improved. In an objective, external way, in the material world of the dice game, his increased winnings corresponded to the decreased possibilities of his movement. And even though he was sure that the outcome of a roll of the dice had nothing to do with whether he had five fingers or four fingers on his hand, Walser looked upon his recent spate of good luck as a mystery, and this mystery bespoke an entrance to another world, a world with which he was yet unfamiliar. For Walser, the connection between those two facts—one less finger, more luck in the dice games—was still incomprehensible and impossible to catalog. Where does one situate the connection? How does one classify the link that existed between these two facts? Which occurrence should Walser classify as the cause and which the effect? And if neither were the cause nor effect of the other, how to classify them, and what other facts could be linked to these two?

To Walser, the opposing hypothesis seemed the most absurd. If he accepted that these two facts weren't connected in any way, but instead depended on other factors, then he would have to accept that his body and existence weren't defined internally, but externally. Did his personal, private luck depend on the war, or the course that it took? Might it depend on the number of dead soldiers or dead insurgents? If this hypothesis were correct, the world would seem even stranger to Walser than it already did.

Such confusion aroused, in Walser, an urgent need to feel safe, which he only felt when he was locked away in his study, in front of his collection. In his study everything was finally whole. There was nothing left to explain. All the pieces of metal were in their proper places on the shelves; they were perfectly coordinated with the records contained in his notebooks, all without a single mistake. Nothing superfluous, nothing missing. And only this precision could comfort him. If the world could be nothing more than his collection, Walser would then have to be described as a happy man—indeed, a powerful one.

However, the occupation continued and—even though the resistance was starting to show signs of weakening—soldiers continued to die. The most significant piece of news was that Ortho—that important military official and war hero, who had already survived a number of assassination attempts—had finally been assassinated. He was killed during his own wedding, by a musician.

The war continued apace: like a lunatic, or maybe like some other thing.

CHAPTER XV

1

Margha Walser wouldn't be considered a pretty woman, but she wasn't completely uninteresting.

Margha had black hair, which was perhaps too long for someone her age, and buttocks that were too big for the average male taste, but her firm-looking breasts compensated for that slightly "unfortunate feature," if one can call it that. She had light-colored eyes, and even though she wasn't a tall woman, she was almost the same height as Walser, which had always sort of bothered her, although she wasn't conscious of it. For Margha, tallness was emblematic of the man who could protect her in any situation.

In those difficult times—on top of which came the reduction of her husband's salary—Margha Walser tried to maintain some sense of stability. Hygiene and nourishment were the two foundations of any home, and Margha Walser didn't tolerate failures in either of these areas. She and her husband had never lacked a robust meal at lunchtime; there were no major luxuries in their household, but nothing essential was ever left out. On top of all her other expenses, she always set aside a small amount that represented two months' worth of future expenditures, and this was a point of pride for her, since it constituted something like a guarantee that they would stay alive, the two of them, she and her husband (at least for the next two months), since they had enough saved to buy food. Her logic could be summed up succinctly in the following formula: "How could we possibly die while we have food?" As if there were no other reason for human death than a lack of food.

2

It was a weekday, Thursday, and after a peaceful dinner at his wife's side, Joseph Walser had, for a few minutes already, been sitting alone at the table, reading his newspaper. Margha Walser appeared at the entryway to the dining room; the sound of her high-heeled shoes disturbed Joseph, and he raised his head. Margha was now standing a few yards away. Wearing makeup, and a skirt she rarely wears.

"Joseph," she said, "may I go out?"

Walser folded his newspaper and stood up from his chair, moving rapidly. He turned his back on his wife, without looking at her, and walked over to the drawer where he kept the key to the study. He took it, opened the door, and entered the study. The sound of the key locking the door from inside was heard.

Inside the study, everything was in its proper place, as always. He pulled out the chair with his right hand and sat down. The empty space that his index finger once occupied no longer disturbed his view in the least. It was as if his hand had been born like that, born together with him.

He opened his notebook and leafed through the few pages of new entries with his right hand. The most recent addition to his collection was a small metal ring, about 1.2 inches across, that he had requested from a woman who was about to put it in the trash.

"What do you want this for? It's useless," the woman had said.

"I'm conducting research," Walser had replied.

The woman's incredulous expression in response to his claim of "research" had no effect on his actions. "I thank you," he had said, "this is a very important piece for me." That piece was now on the desk in his study, right in front of him.

Walser felt a certain perplexity with regard to the piece of metal. He had already recorded all of its dimensions, he'd already made a precise drawing of it, and also recorded the place and the circumstances in which he had "found" it, but something essential was lacking: What mechanism did that piece belong to? At the time, he had asked the woman and she didn't know the answer: "It was left in the doorway of our building. I don't know where it came from. Maybe from the war."

The metal ring didn't look like it belonged to any domestic object. In fact, it could be a part of a weapon or some sort of military device.

For Walser, the most fascinating parts of this work were those moments when he felt like he was doing "research." Where did this piece come from? What mechanism had made it function? Or, to pose that question another way: what mechanism no longer functioned as a result of missing this piece, which had been abandoned in front of a building? Yes, there was no doubt about it: this piece of metal had belonged to a weapon.

Walser took great pleasure in this idea. If that piece belonged to a weapon, be it large or small, it would no longer be able to function now, since the piece in question was right there, in front of him, on his desk, just inches from his hands.

Looking down again at the piece of metal, he felt that he was interfering in the war. There's a weapon that can't fire because I have one of its parts right here! For the first time, he felt like he was a part of something: he was participating. Furthermore: he felt that it—the war—had finally become important to him. He, Joseph Walser, was touching, with his undamaged left hand and his right hand with its missing finger—the index finger—a weapon; he possessed, at that moment, in his very hands, an indispensable part of the conflict. He had interrupted the war.

An absurd thought even popped into his head, that he should start stealing a piece, albeit a tiny one, from each weapon in the city, and thus, through almost imperceptible means, put an end to all the bother. "A one-man conspiracy," said Walser, and he couldn't stop smiling at how ridiculous the idea was.

But he really was interrupting the war, there was no doubt about it in his mind. By recording the data from that piece of metal, by adding it to his collection, he was removing it from the world, removing it from the reach of other men's actions. And a question subsequently arose: which side did the weapon—the one that he had interrupted, so to speak—belong to? Which side? The army of the occupation? The guerrillas? And, ultimately, what did it matter?

He finally understood his precise position in relation to the formidable events taking place in the city: What did it matter who the weapon belonged to? The answer wasn't relevant. He had merely acquired a new specimen for his collection.

Meanwhile, he heard a noise. It was the front door. Margha had just left.

Joseph Walser slid the ruler across the desk with his right hand. He had to confirm the width of the piece of metal, but his right hand was shaking.

CHAPTER XVI

1

Having just finished his shift a few minutes earlier, Joseph Walser was gathering his things before he went home when he received a visit from Klober, the foreman, with whom he hadn't crossed paths for a number of weeks.

"Joseph Walser, it's good to see you!"

The two men shook hands, with Klober, as usual, being the more forceful of the two.

"I can see that it's getting better, it's not so red anymore," said Klober, looking at Walser's hand. "The body gets accustomed to things, doesn't it?"

Joseph said nothing.

"My dear Walser, I came here specifically to see you. I'm paying you a visit, if that's what you'd like to call it. I'm fond of you, it's undeniable. And even the distance that our different positions have created between us hasn't extinguished my fondness for you. How can I explain it? There are a number of reasons, some of which aren't very concrete or logical, but there are others that you know quite well.

"I want you to know that I was dismayed by your accident. I wouldn't go as far as to say that it changed my life, you know me well enough to know that neither hypocrisy nor feigned concern is really my style. My dear Walser, we're both men, and my life, obviously, has to go on.

"You might think that I took pleasure in your accident, but when we shook hands just moments before, I felt a very strong connection between the two substances involved: my hand and yours. It seems strange, but that's life: strangeness; until the very last instant: strangeness.

"But let's move on: Walser, I have a certain fondness for you— let me repeat—a certain irrational fondness for you, so much so that it puts me at risk. That's why I want to tell you quickly what I came here to say. I have important information. I advise you to forget about the dice game tomorrow night at your good friend Fluzst's house. Certain friendships are problematic, my dear Walser, but it's our heart that decides who we'll be friends with— as our beloved Romantics would say—not us. Well then, it's time to put some other organs to use, if I may put it that way. It's not the time for intuitive gut feelings to take responsibility for our actions. The head, Walser, we live in a time when the head is the most important organ, so to speak. We must keep it raised higher than the rest of one's organism, you see? Higher. In tumultuous times, hierarchies should be preserved at all cost: the head, as you, my good sir, have certainly already noticed, was placed in a privileged position, if we can call it that, upon the human organism. On top, you see? Right up top. Of course, sometimes it would almost be better if our brains were located in some other part of our organism, some place that's better protected. I just came in from the street, Walser, and I saw a body, the body of a man— now hardly a man at all, I would say—with his head disfigured, a soldier whose head had been disfigured by two bullets. And it's at moments like those when you realize that our intelligence should be better protected, it should have been placed somewhere down low, not up top, where it's so visible. But, as you can plainly see: there's no solution.

"Still, while we're still alive on this magnificent earth, which we undoubtedly love unequivocally, you and I, so much so that we'd be willing to die for it—isn't that right, Walser, my friend? Well then, when the country seems like it is falling to pieces, at those times, at these times, we should simply protect the organs that enable us to perceive the world; and you know very well which ones those are.

"The rest of it doesn't concern us.

"But forgive me for going on like this, it's just that I'm overjoyed to see you again, and the presence of my good friend Walser lets my rational mind loose; I feel eloquent when I'm by your side. Well then, here is the important information, once more; an extremely important piece of information: tomorrow, Saturday, forget about that dice game! Tomorrow night they're going to arrest Fluzst. That man has gotten himself into a disastrous mess.

"I know that Fluzst is your friend, or some such similar thing, and, by the way, I've never known you to have any others; you, my good sir, aren't an easy man to get along with, as you must know, and you've developed very few relationships. We all belong to the same world and the same eternity, if I may use that word, so we should get to know each other better, don't you think? Maybe that way we'd be able to love one another, who knows?

"There's one day left, enough time for you to leave here and warn Fluzst. Or, on the other hand, you can take my advice: just forget about your dice game tomorrow. From what I've heard, you haven't won that much anyway, and money isn't the only thing that keeps us alive, as you must have already realized.

"My dear Walser, it's such a pity, but I really have to say good-bye. It was good to see you again, and it's always a pleasure to do so. I forgot to mention that the information I gave you is completely confidential, not even your adorable wife should know about it. Consider this a test of your personality. You have one day, more than twenty-four hours in front of you, to prove your convictions and intelligence. Once again I hold my right hand out to you; hold yours out to me as well. My dear Walser, I'm counting on you."

CHAPTER XVII

1

Saturday night the city takes on an odd logic; a schizoid personality becomes readily apparent in men who are able to move straight from their loathsome days into occupying themselves, remorselessly, with nonstop dancing and dim, arousing lights. People are having fun.

A boyfriend and girlfriend are guessing at sentences that the other makes up. It's a game: he writes something down on a piece of paper, then hides what he's written; she guesses what it is, and they compare the two; they laugh at the results, whenever they're completely different, laugh at the predictability or unpredictability of their ideas.

Moving successively, purposelessly, the woman's elbows manage to knock over a glass of wine; she bursts out laughing, and the man apologizes to their waiter and says that he'll pay for everything.

Hidden passions are revealed by reckless kisses. Formulaic amorous phrases are repeated, sentences copied from someone else, but which, when spoken or heard in isolation, become essential, capable of occupying a person's thoughts for an entire week. In times of little imagination a new science is constructed: the formulation of love in a series of phrases: like an experimental study in which one already knows, with absolute certainty, what practical effects or moral consequences certain phrases have on the body of a man or a woman on a Saturday night. A night when the city, protected as it is by soldiers, seems inaccessible to death, which has a way of humbling the joys of even the victorious or indifferent.

Periods of great fear are good for more than just survival: they're also good for passion. But if the quality of an entire generation can be measured by the quality of the phrases that its seducers utilize, then this generation, without a doubt, was a mediocre one.

Inseparable from a certain violence (as if it were its counterpoint), these seductions are made up, on these particular nights, of well-aimed blows, so to speak, that hit their targets in that part of existence which lies outside oneself. In every moment of respite from serious illness or fear, people head out to the streets, people sing; adolescents spy through keyholes to inspect the limits of their morality as well as the unashamed nudity of their housemaids; after advancing decisively through unsafe locations, soldiers learn dance-steps, useless steps, though steps that could, nevertheless, efficiently seduce even the most resolute women; the soldiers listen to their dance instructor the way they used to listen to the officers who taught them other sorts of steps, another way to walk across this earth.

Since an explanation of all existence can't fit on a single table-top, two soldiers opt instead for more beers, which fit nicely, and their dates can't stop smiling, drunk, their bladders full and their breasts swollen. People leave their houses to search for perfection and, indeed, they find soldiers—whose deadly weapons seem reduced now to a mere detail in their wardrobe—and even find women who've been abandoned by their courageous or dead husbands, and who, confused, mix incompatible styles in their chosen attire, as well as in their fluctuating demeanors: meaningful stares, typical of prostitutes, accompanying phrases spoken using absolutely perfect, refined grammar, voicing their eloquent anxieties about the "instability of the current political situation." The women are debasing themselves. These men are from other cities; they're merely passing through.

But joy doesn't yield. The two lovers endeavor to inaugurate a new century, one belonging solely to their table: a private century. A stupid woman, with her ill-mannered elbows on the table, and with her dress already marked by two wine stains, that woman, who earlier in the afternoon was disparaging the humanity of people whose names she can't even spell, is now rubbing her high-heeled shoe against a soldier's boot, emulating the behavior of people she's seen in films; and she's already feeling a certain sort of feminine desire begin to express itself in the area above her knees.

Normality continues apace; no one disturbs it, as there's a constant need to keep moving, which, from a distance, seems incomprehensible, almost absurd. Normality continues trudging apace, even on top of ruins; the human organism endeavors to maintain its habits, even in the strangest and most confusing situations. Men do not stop for a single minute, whether they're satisfied or trying to adapt to a new element; indeed, this is the reason that they get out of bed. And since they have desires they'll never stop searching. Searching for what? That which has been stolen from them.

It was in the midst of this *urgency of normality* that emerges at the most dynamic times, those days whose borders most readily allow for important actions to be taken within them—as if time contained a specific volume, which can be either volatile or concentrated—it was in the midst of this urgency that the dice game, for example, was organized, the game that Joseph Walser participated in every Saturday night. The game was a habit that predated the soldiers' invasion of the city, and had continued afterward, without any significant changes.

The rules of an autonomous world, a closed world, do not change, especially when unpredictability occupies a central place in each day in the outside world.

In opposition to the administration of their country, every man in time of war, individually, on his own, founded, as it were, a Ministry of Normality, which established, essentially, repetitions. Because only repetitions calmed their minds, only repetitions allowed each individual to wake up to find themselves human the next day. Repetitions of small actions or small gestures, of banal words or phrases—even repetitions of invisible acts, acts that weren't noted by other people, like repeated images and memories in one's brain, all of which allowed each person to survive in the midst of chaos, stand fast in the midst of the reigning disorder, in the midst of that which Klober was wont to call *a century of unpredictability*, a century that wasn't merely opposed to repetition, but was the *enemy of repetition*. "This is not a normal century," Klober often said, "but men in this century are still the same as they always were." And that was it, that mixture: these were men who had been invaded while repeating the essential actions of generations past—and this is a precise use of the word *invaded*, for it describes both the directional flow and the speed of the movements under discussion—and, through this invasion, found themselves invaded as well by completely new phenomena.

"No prophet ever so much as correctly predicted the color of shoes in our century," mocked Klober.

2

The city was bustling, and the sounds from the Saturday night revelry were coming in through the windows of Margha and Joseph Walser's house.

Margha looked at the clock in the living room and then at her husband.

"It's already nine o'clock. What about your game?"

"I'm not going today," said Joseph Walser.

3

On that Saturday night three men were arrested in Fluzst's house. Fluzst himself, Normaas, and Rolph. Normaas and Rolph were arrested on charges of "knowledge of important information" and "friendship with members of the resistance." At four o'clock in the afternoon on Sunday, Fluzst was executed by a firing squad.

On that night, of the five regular dice players, both Joseph Walser and Strumm were missing. These two men had disrupted their normality by not showing up, as was their habit, at Fluzst's house.

Seated around the table, Fluzst, Normaas, and Rolph began to think that Joseph and Strumm's lateness was odd. Their lateness was, after a certain point, "surprising," given that neither of the two had sent word. When they heard someone knocking on the door, the feeling of oddity disappeared and the sensation of normality was, for a few moments, restored. Normaas was the one who, with his customary good nature, went to answer the door. He opened it with a joke in his head about the two missing players' unpunctuality. He never got to say anything. It was the soldiers.

The night would no longer be normal. Confusion had invaded the few hours that the dice players had previously managed to protect from the century going on in the outside world. You can't escape the century, each of the men must have thought, at the moment when the eight soldiers pointed their guns at each of their terrified human heads.

CHAPTER XVIII

1

Months after the execution, Joseph Walser passed by Fluzst's widow in the street. The city had been through so many disturbing days that this one tragic, albeit limited, individual event seemed, even to the people closest to it, to have appeared and disappeared many years before.

"How have you been?" Walser greeted her politely.

Fluzst's widow had stopped wearing her mourning clothes some time ago. She was wearing a long, gray skirt from which projected a robust feminine backside; her breasts were also ample. Clairie had gained a few pounds since the "event," as everyone, out of a sense of propriety, called Fluzst's execution (or occasionally as: "the thing that happened"); those ample breasts seemed to want to escape from the inside of her white shirt, and caused some intense disquiet in Walser.

Clairie was a woman who had always stimulated his curiosity. She was extremely circumspect, said very little, only what was necessary, responding solicitously to any request her husband made; aside from all this, Clairie played an important role on the nights when they held the game in which Walser had participated for years.

Any of his previous, more prolonged glances at her had, nevertheless, been filtered through and annulled by a situation that was completely different from the present one; a fixed situation, one could call it, a situation that, in and of itself, didn't give any indication of the changes which were imminent, and thus presented itself to Joseph Walser as an eternal situation; a situation in which this woman—Clairie—the wife of the man of the house—the aforementioned Fluzst—often brought a bottle of homemade wine into the game room, which reinvigorated the players and allowed for a small interruption of the greed that gradually took hold of them through the evening. It was the entrance of a woman into the room, together with the wine, let's say, that allowed for a certain emotional restraint to be practiced, in the game. The instinctual and borderline dangerous avarice that accumulated with each roll of the dice was suddenly diverted in another direction, thanks simply to the introduction of a feminine element into the space. A strong, unexpected downpour on a day when the forecast had called for mild weather wouldn't produce a greater surprise than the one brought about by the entrance of this woman, Clairie, into the game room. She was the conspicuous infiltration of another world, a prompt reminder that the outside world never failed to send to the five players. Her entrance halfway through the game, with wine and sometimes pieces of bread, in spite of her discretion, her reticence, was like an indication that there was still a war on, in that it represented, for the players, an "awakening."

However, the situation was now completely different. It was fixed in a new way, a new eternity seemed to have been established: the woman was now a widow; which is to say that the woman— Clairie—no longer had a man at her side. And she was still young, this woman who passed by Walser on the street on that late afternoon, wearing a white blouse, not transparent, but a blouse in which her breasts were, so to speak, a powerful element, an element that disturbed the unequivocal way that Walser tended to look at her. The contour of her especially robust right breast, due to some oversight or impulsive movement on her part, was now faintly visible; this contour became an obsession for Walser.

"Are you still working in the clerks' office, Mr. Walser?"

Joseph responded by nodding his head and smiling. Clairie also worked for a company owned by Leo Vast. During the day, the two of them went through the same sorts of movements and followed the same sorts of ritual.

"Companions in slavery," joked Walser.

Clairie smiled.

After a few brief words, Clairie said good-bye. Joseph Walser didn't move a single foot forward; he turned around and stood watching the movement of Clairie's buttocks as she walked away. Without spending even a second on formulating a plan, Walser, excited, took a few small, quick steps toward Clairie (while at the same time instinctively hiding his deformed right hand at the side of his body) and called out to her, in a tone of voice that, in a different situation, would have filled him with shame.

"Ms. Clairie!"

Clairie stopped and turned around. She smiled.

"Yes?"

Walser was absolutely overwrought and, sensing some encouragement in her smile, whispered:

"Ms. Clairie, I need to say something to you, something that I've kept hidden for a long time. Something that has to do with my affections, Ms. Clairie, something that has to do with powerful feelings."

2

"Behave yourself, Mr. Walser. We're in the middle of the street," said Clairie. "Certain things should never be said to a woman regardless of the situation, much less in this one. My husband just recently died, and you, sir, were one of his friends. I'm still in mourning."

And then, suddenly, she asked:

"Mr. Walser, why didn't you show up for the game that night?"

Walser didn't respond. Clairie turned around and quickly walked away.

"Stupid woman," murmured Joseph Walser, before taking one last look at the movement of Clairie's buttocks.

Meanwhile, two soldiers came up to him.

Joseph straightened his posture, proceeded to perform a protracted and respectful gesture in their direction, and only then started off again.

CHAPTER XIX

1

The danger of the current situation had a visible effect on the suppression of individual personalities—in their prominence. "Any man who lets himself get too close to current circumstances," Klober sometimes said, "might end up engaged in the conversation."

Every event that became fixed in one's individual memory was, for Klober, nothing less than the remote consequence of a balancing act: you see, the acts of living beings, beings endowed with a degree of intellectual willpower, so to speak, either interfere with immovable objects, or not; and from this interaction between two worlds there must follow a specific result, naturally, an objective effect that—if only there were methods for measuring practical experience scientifically, methods as refined as those that operate in certain laboratories—could even be expressed by a concrete, a precise number, one that would be immediately understood everywhere. But since such was not the case—that is, since individual perception resists codification into an objective science able to observe and explain its inner workings, each individual memory remains just that: individual, different from any other; indeed, marked by a retreat from others. If a collective shared the exact same memory, it wouldn't be a collective; it would be a single unit of existence. Therefore, to speak about the collective memory of a nation is simple foolishness—but is, at the same time, an excellent political strategy. The History being taught to children was obviously an attempt to establish a formula dictating the organization of memory in those young minds: one that was both limited and quantitative. Learning the History of a country means—if you're paying attention—losing your individual memory. "It's being taught History that first begins to destroy a citizen," said Klober. "It's no surprise that not a single genius has been born in the last fifty years: who can be creative, truly creative, when he is inebriated with History from an early age?

"My dear Walser," insisted Klober, "none of those events occurred in the way that they're talked about, it's impossible for any verbal description to evoke or explain organic events. Not even images can do it."

The country was equipped with only two witnesses, each replete with equivocations: neither eyes nor language could hope to perceive even the minimal laws of existence. Two witnesses—eyes and language—that deceive.

Events occur alone, apart from us, uncomprehended; deep down, they are solitary beings—please excuse the ridiculous metaphor, but that's precisely what they are: no event has ever been perceived to date. From the most significant, national events to the most discreet episodes of an individual's life: we do not yet have a science that can truly perceive what happens or what has happened. The very precondition of the scientific method destroys the possibility of such objective observation taking place: that absurd idea, still defended, that science is universal, that it must be understood by all individuals in the same way. That meager rendering of causes and effects, those rows of numbers, the crowding in of explanations of some occurrence now reduced to numbers or letters. They stuff a series of individual, unrepeatable facts into a formula and present it to the entire world, saying: here is what happened to a certain man at a specific time and location, here is the summary of it, for all to understand. And, if possible, it is made into Law, or History.

In truth, we really understand very little, or nothing at all, because we reject the idea of an individualized science, of a science that is both geographically and temporally personalized. Since this individual science, although truly necessary, is useless to one's country, to the world—assuming such things really exist— and since, furthermore, it's dangerous, because nothing is more divisive than explaining the same event in different ways—and it would end up dividing the very thing that a nation would want to unite: Mankind—the idea of an individual science was, right from the start, made to seem pointless: it isn't necessary, it's superfluous, it's harmful, it should be eliminated, and eventually, as a final measure, forgotten. "These days," said Klober, "is there anyone who even remembers that anyone might have proposed the development of an individualized science, a science that always comes with a first name attached to it, and that doesn't bother to engage with any other mode of reason?

"An individualized science," said Klober, "an isolated explanation of phenomena is, indeed, urgently needed.

"Struggling by oneself is a laudable act, but it depends as much on the particularities of one's strength as it does the particularities of one's mind. A crazy person can struggle by himself all he likes, or a man devoid of all capacity to reason; likewise a man with a mediocre intelligence, let him toil away on his own. But a solitary explanation for phenomena requires a different altitude—let's use that word—of intelligence. Every creative instinct begins with this primeval necessity, which the collective memory would have us forget: we're creative because we want to find a solitary explanation, an individual explanation, an explanation that has no equal, that has no duplicate, that is impossible to follow—a selfish explanation, some will say, yes, a selfish explanation, of course. To go even further: it's hateful: it's an explanation that hates other explanations, that fights against them; but it doesn't battle them merely to defeat these other explanations, no, it does it to defeat, vanquish, and eliminate the very men who harbor other solitary explanations! The solitary explanation, which is individualized science *par excellence*, at its most extreme, seeks to eliminate all other beings, because it hates them; it hates them simply because any other intelligence, any other possibility for solitude, are proof that we do not inhabit this world alone.

"There is only one true non-collective being, or asocial being, as it's sometimes called. And this being isn't someone who isolates itself, isn't someone who runs off into the mountains or the forest, no, it is a being that kills other beings, the one who wants to kill all other ones so it can finally be alone: this is the true solitary being. The other ones, the ones that run off into the mountains or the forest, they're not solitary beings at all: they're cowards. The same goes for those who won't leave their houses until the war is over. Don't leave the forest until your life is over: this is the brilliant formula that some sages have used to resolve the question of existence! No, my dear Walser, you're either ready to hate other people as much as possible or you should have never bothered to become strong in the first place, for, you see, you are not yet sufficiently individual. Hatred is the great emblem of Man, of his true particularity, his display of difference, his separation from other things. It is your hatred that gives you your name. Your mother, your father—those who provided you with your body—will only recognize you by your hatred. Let's not allow ourselves to be deceived by morality or by the History of a country, which, deep down, are two identical forces: morality and History are just two ways that the collective, your country, tells you, or asks you, to cease to exist. Cease to exist, says the collective morality!

"And that is where war comes into play, as you must have already noticed," continued Klober, "for war comes closer than anything to the true nature of Man, and that's why people are so frightened by it. But this war, like all the others, still isn't man's ultimate truth, it still isn't a procedure that's capable of completely eliminating the possibility of deceit; the final war, the true one, far removed from the mere imitation before us, will be one in which each man battles against every other man, in which each man will make up the entirety of his own individual army; the true war, the precise war, the war that will finally demonstrate what it is to be an individual, that war, which has not yet taken place, which has barely been dreamed of, but which shall come, I'm sure of it, that war is one in which any two bodies that approach each other will do so out of hate. Any two people who approach one another will do so in order to kill—or else we will still have yet to see true Men."

CHAPTER XX

1

Not six months had passed since their brief, unpleasant conversation, when Clairie, on some flimsy pretext, asked Walser to pay a visit to her house, which, for a single woman, at once revealed an abrupt diminution of her sense of propriety.

The widow had taken down all the photographs of Fluzst. There wasn't a single trace of her former husband.

"I've made some changes to the house," said Clairie, "I wanted you to see it, Mr. Walser."

Walser looked all around him. Clairie moved toward him.

"I hope you aren't upset with me, Mr. Walser. I was too harsh with you that day."

Clairie moved even closer to him. Walser whispered:

"Margha is expecting me."

Clairie leaned towards Walser's face and kissed it.

"I hope you'll drop by often, the way you used to," she said.

2

On his way home—after that first kiss from Clairie—Joseph Walser was thinking about something else. On some other plane of existence, we might say.

He was excited, but this excitement came from inside him. Walser couldn't stop thinking about something that Klober had said in public once, in front of four or five men, with an expression on his face that made it seem as though he was taking great pride in having the courage to say such things:

"The great mass murderers in History didn't hate enough. There was always someone on their side. They were never truly alone," Klober had said.

"They possessed what any rational man would have to call 'an unfinished hatred,' or 'an incomplete hatred.'

"No," Klober had said, "that is not enough."

CHAPTER XXI

1

Something had recently become very clear to Walser: he was not a Great Man. He didn't even need any proof: the contrary assertion had never even reached the stage of hypothesis; as such, this fact was essentially an encumbrance imposed upon him by existence: he was a common man, a man that belonged to a never-ending species that had roamed the world for centuries, replete with new ideas and instruments.

This expression frightened him a little; thus, he paused before it as if it were an object—a material, concrete obstacle blocking his way; there it is again: *an endless species*. He, Joseph Walser, by virtue of being a common man, belonged to an endless species. And, oh, how it frightened him to think about that *endlessness*. He almost whispered, pathetically: I want to get off. Because, in fact, it sometimes seemed to him impossible to get off, to *abandon this endlessness*. How can I depart from it?

From an early age it had been clear to him that he didn't want to be a protagonist, just a witness. And his difficulty with existence lay in precisely this concrete problem: on many occasions Walser had seen himself, from a distance, being happy; just as he had also observed, from a distance, his own sadness or exasperation. Nothing more. But he was never able to get *outside* of his own indifference; to get outside of himself in those innumerable moments when he found himself neutral in front of everything, inert and simply waiting when faced with the possibility of some action or its reverse. The more excitement contained in his body, the easier it was to distance himself, to be a witness of himself. The difficulties with this privileged observation—this observation of an existence that was nominally his own—arose, then, most powerfully, when the intensity of his feelings was almost null. If he was already unable to get *there*—outside himself, yet still within existence—how would he ever be able to distance himself farther still? And what, in concrete terms, was this *there*, this other place that sometimes seemed to be the very center of his being and at other times its periphery? As to the general location of this *there*, Walser didn't have a doubt about it: it was his brain. It was there that everything took place, or where everything that took place was observed. Everything was done there, and everything that was done was observed there. Just like for any average lunatic, thought Walser, and he smiled at this formulation.

Indeed, he was one Man among endless men, a common Man; but how many great men were there? How many great men had there been during the century that was coming to a close? And would we even know how to count them? Would we have an arithmetic sufficient to detect their greatness and quantify it? Would all those men turn out to be public figures, men whose individual acts had prevented catastrophes or created them, or else hastened their occurrence? Could a great man go unrecognized as such by his closest neighbor? A great man in disguise, an anonymous great man? A great man who was merely a gardener?

Walser smiled.

What intrigued him was the fact that he, Joseph Walser, had no aspirations in that regard. He *didn't want* to be a Great Man. And that was unusual, for he sensed in people—in almost everyone—a hidden, unremitting force that drove them to their actions, as mediocre as these might be, filled with a different sort of passion—that's the word we'll use—as if never wavering for a second in their conviction that, sooner or later, the magnificent destiny that awaited them would reveal itself in the light of day, for all to see—from their neighbors to the farthest-flung fellow citizen—and this destiny was this and this alone: to be a Great Man.

As he proceeded down the street and passed people by, Walser looked timidly at each of their faces and thought: is it possible that this man has no desire to be a great man?

And this question seemed very odd to him, and any response to it quite unacceptable—as was the inverse question: is it possible that this man here, who at this moment is crossing paths with me on the street, is it possible that this shapeless face, which I don't recognize, and which doesn't show any hint of hiding any special characteristics or exceptional strength, is it possible, all told, that this face, which is basically a repetition of countless other faces, that this *endless* face, which is grotesquely common-place, is it possible that behind this face there is a man who desires to be great, and who believes that such a thing might still be possible?

2

Walser then remembered the words of Klober, the man who was sleeping with his wife, and who calmly continued to utter grand phrases in his presence, as if he were constantly on a stage delivering a speech. All the things that Klober had said about the hatred that was the real requisite for greatness and the isolation that such hatred presupposes, all that now seemed untrue to Walser. A Great Man, or at least the ones who are considered to be great men, always wants to be admired; that is to say: he's not so strong that he doesn't still desire the attention of others. If he is admired, it's because he desired it. And Klober wanted to be a Great Man; when he made his impassioned speeches, what he really wanted was to be admired. He spoke of a prideful, self-imposed solitude, but in speaking about these things—by not having restricted himself to merely thinking them, keeping them inside his private, non-exhibitionist circuitry—by speaking about them publicly, he was contradicting himself. The very act of speaking those phrases contradicted the message they conveyed.

But concerning himself, Walser was now intrigued, for the first time, in an objective way, by his indifference to receiving any applause or cheers for his actions. If he were being completely realistic about it, Walser would have had to admit that no action he had initiated throughout his entire existence had yielded the slightest cheer—indeed, neither insult nor applause. Even when he was reprimanded, even when he was humiliated, Walser had never felt any hatred directed specifically at him. No one hated him. And that fact could as easily make him feel ashamed as, on the contrary, give him an elevated sense of security. In certain epochs, like the one in which he was living, it was reassuring to think that no one, in any place, was, at that moment, recalling one's name or one's face with hatred. Walser had never committed a single act that even an ingenuous child would call mischief. He just wasn't fit for doing evil, thought Walser, as if this were a clearly delineated ineptitude, like any other defective mechanism. He wasn't hated and he felt hatred for no one. When he performed an action he never looked around to see whether this had been admired or not. The effects of his actions weren't important.

Certainly he thought that the immediate effects of his movements, for instance, were important, for they were parts of his concrete life, to put it one way—or rather, to put it more simply, if he decided to jump off a tall building, he knew, or anyway suspected, that this would result in his death; therefore: he didn't jump. And it was this type of reasoning that attached itself to his individual actions—merely: what will happen to me, and only me, after I do this? Everything else was meaningless to him: if people admired or rejected a series of his movements, or the sum total of his gestures—his behavior, in other words—it was all the same to him.

For Walser, it had become clear that one's existence was made up of a succession of behaviors directed at objects and at other men, and that these behaviors, these ways of acting—crude as they might be—were, objectively speaking, nothing more than a series of clearly delineated movements taken by one's musculature, easily located on an anatomic chart. The biography of a Man was, at root, merely the movements that his muscles had made.

Each individual event could thus be, not reduced, but likened to—the question was one of equivalence, identity, not of reduction or a loss—the sum total of one's gestures, the way that a machine—as complex as it might be, as marvelous as its actions might be—is nevertheless nothing more than the sum total of its parts, which, under certain circumstances, perform actions. Walser didn't think it right for Man—purely by virtue of being able to reflect upon the mechanisms of his existence—to pride himself on being so very different from machines. Merely being able to distance oneself from one's constituent mechanisms doesn't mean that those mechanisms cease to exist. Thus, a human existence was, for Walser, a simple sum. The mathematical *plus* sign reigned in all living beings, and death was so dreadfully frightening precisely because it represented an abrupt interruption of the arithmetic that, at some level, everyone was made to think would go on forever. As if each person, at a given moment, conceived of his body in these terms: as *an immortal summation of various behaviors.* No one in this century, even after so many successive generations had come and gone—even in the middle of a war, when death is more visible than ever—had ever failed to be surprised (Walser was certain of this) by their own death. We're always surprised! As if we believed we had the right, after so many days of continued existence, to never be interrupted; as if we had the basic right to belong to a completely different species, to a legitimately *never-ending* species. This is more than just a belief in an individual eternity in the abstract; this is a belief in an eternity with our own name on it, an eternity that attaches itself to our singular existence.

And then Walser couldn't help but get caught up in a sense of pride: he, yes he, was a Great Man after all, a Man, as Klober contended, who had been able to separate himself from everyone else, a Man who was truly alone and individual. Precisely because his actions didn't seem to have any connection to other people— as if those other people didn't exist. They were absolutely separate, he and other people; his actions were independent, autonomous, and that was his greatness. In short, there was, in Walser, at last, a generalized hatred, a hatred that was serene yet universal, a hatred directed at each and every individual that crossed paths with his existence.

And yet, he would never be an emperor; History would never, regarding Walser, tell of the way he had exterminated this or that number of his fellow human beings, because he, Walser, would never get close to anyone. He was not yet the true Man, as Klober had put it, the Man who only ventures near other people in order to kill them; but, nevertheless, there was still something very significant in Walser: his every point of proximity to other existences, even if these weren't approached with the intention of *killing* the other person, were, by nature, and had been for some time, taken up with the intention *of not loving* the other person. I can draw near to anyone with perfect security, thought Walser, remembering the kiss he'd given Clairie, I can draw near to anyone without fear because I know I won't love them. *I am prepared to not love anyone*—and this sentence, thought in this way, felt like a powerful weapon—in wartime—a powerful defense against the hostility of the century. Walser didn't even own a pistol, but he had eliminated the great weakness of existence, he had made the principal fragility of the species disappear: he had no inclination toward love or friendship! And in that moment, while walking down the street, unarmed, looking down at his old, brown shoes, his irresponsible shoes, as Klober used to say mockingly, at that moment Walser felt as safe—and at the same time as threatening to others—as if he were proceeding down the street in a tank.

However, he suddenly jumped to the side. He had almost stepped on a large, amorphous mass. It was a man. And he was dead.

CHAPTER XXII

1

Someone had purposefully placed the man there. Sometimes soldiers would leave the bodies of guerrillas or conspirators out in the middle of the road—for some time, even days on end—for the whole population to see.

The corpse was lying face down and the blood on the asphalt beside its head was already dry. He had been killed there, at this exact spot.

No uniform: he was wearing black pants, a black belt, and a gray shirt. Walser bent over slightly to see his face. Maybe it was someone he knew. He bent over some more: nope, no one he knew. It was a man. Just a man, he murmured.

The man didn't have any shoes on. Certainly someone had stolen them from him. The world goes on, and this detail, the absurd absence of the man's shoes, proved it. Someone had stolen from the corpse.

And now Walser felt pride for his city. It goes on, it endures, it survives. It's intelligent, this city, he thought.

He wasn't ashamed; Walser hadn't felt that kind of propriety for some time. There was a corpse on the street that no longer needed shoes: someone had stolen them; all was well. It would be irrational to leave shoes there, on a dead man's feet. An intelligent city, he thought again.

Meanwhile, some people passed by; one of them walked over and looked at the corpse. "Another one," the man said; Walser nodded in agreement and the man walked away. Another person came close by but didn't slow down; he said nothing and maintained his pace.

Joseph Walser kept looking. He looked at the corpse's hands. First at the left hand, then at the right hand. The dead man's palms were facing up.

Instinctively, Walser counted the fingers on each hand. Five fingers. Two perfect, complete hands. More than that: they were clean: without a single spot of blood or dirt on them. Clean and normal. The hands of a living man, you could say.

He kept looking at the dead man's perfectly intact fingers. He smiled, and had the urge to say out loud, to anyone who was a part of that silent spectacle: How can a man be dead if his hands are still intact? How can he be dead if he has five fingers on each hand?

He laughed to himself at the absurdity of it. An obscene affront to existence and events: the corpse had two perfect hands!

Another thought passed through Walser's head: just as the thief had stolen the dead man's shoes, Walser could snatch the dead man's right hand, take it with him, and switch it with his own. What would the dead man want with all those fingers, since he's already dead?

Walser looked around him, as if to see if anyone was watching, and, for a second, felt like his plan was viable: he would steal the dead man's right hand and run off.

But no, it wasn't possible; in that situation, jealousy was a waste of emotion. The man was dead; Walser was not in fact confronted with this man, even though he was only a few inches away. "He's gone," said Walser.

A very sensible word to use when speaking of a dead person: *gone*, gone away from here. The man had taken a trip. But how is it that someone so passive could travel? *Travel after death*—Walser tried to smile.

But then a minor detail caught his attention: the belt. The corpse's back was facing him, so only the back of the belt was visible, but it would certainly have a buckle.

His thoughts had already embarked down another path, they had been normalized, if we can put it that way. The shock of coming upon a corpse in the middle of the street had worn off. Walser's organism had returned to normalcy.

He was now observing different details, his attention was elsewhere: his collection didn't contain a single piece that had belonged to a corpse that he'd seen with his own eyes. And there it was: the corpse. And one with a belt; a belt that certainly had a metal buckle. Walser was now concentrated on how to steal the belt from the corpse, right there, in the middle of the street.

He looked around: nobody there. He bent over impulsively and pushed the corpse onto its right side; it was easy; he pushed harder and was able to roll the corpse over completely. Its face had been disfigured by a bullet, but Walser barely even glanced at it. He stood up again, straightened his back, and looked around. Someone was walking toward him from the end of the street. Walser stood still.

The corpse was now face up. One side of his face was deformed, but there were still some individual features left. Walser looked at the dead man's face. A stranger, that one.

Meanwhile, the person at the end of the street had walked over to him.

"It never stops," said the man.

Walser didn't respond, and the man bent over to take a closer look at the corpse's face.

"A bullet," he said. "Do you know him?"

Walser responded that he did not.

"May I ask you for a favor," Walser asked suddenly. "It's his belt. Can you help me?"

"That's stealing," said the man. "I'm a soldier."

Walser was now frightened.

"This man is dead," he said.

"Even so. It's theft of private property."

The two of them were alone. They remained quiet for a few seconds.

"Don't be afraid. I'll help you," said the man, finally.

". . . just need you to lift the torso," said Walser.

Walser bent down and began to unfasten the belt. The other man also leaned over the corpse and lifted its torso a few inches off the ground, so that Joseph could pull the belt through its loops. But the man soon let go of the body, without warning.

"It's heavy."

They both stood up; someone was coming.

2

It was a woman. She didn't stop. On the contrary: she picked up her pace.

The two of them bent over again, and again the man lifted the torso of the corpse off the ground. Walser pulled on the belt and finally removed it. The man sat the corpse back down. "It's heavy," he repeated, while brushing off his hands.

Walser thanked him and rolled up the belt.

"What's your name?"
"Joseph Walser," Walser replied, embarrassed.
"Hinnerk Obst," said the other man, introducing himself.
The two men shook hands.

CHAPTER XXIII

1

For the last few days, Joseph Walser had sensed something strange going on with his wife. They spoke very little; communication between them had always been difficult—neither of them was much of a talker, and what did they have to say to each other anyway? However, it had grown worse over the last three days. During that time, Margha had said, at most, and in a hushed voice, "yes," here or there, in response to concrete requests.

Joseph, however, had been locked in his study for hours, excited. He had already removed the buckle from the rest of the belt, which he'd thrown in the trash, drawn the sketch of the piece in his notebook, and recorded all its measurements. Under the column marked "location," Walser had written: Dokrement Blukn Street; under "time" he'd written: 7:30 P.M.; under "function": buckle belonging to a black leather belt (to fasten/unfasten it); and under "Other Particularities" he'd written, with a certain pride: "Taken off the body of a corpse, with the assistance of Mr. Hinnerk Obst."

Joseph Walser shut the door to his study, locking it with his key from the outside, as usual, and walked into the living room: Margha was crying.

"What's the matter?"

Margha wiped her face; and after a brief silence, softly said:

"It's Klober. He said he doesn't want me anymore."

PART III

CHAPTER XXIV

1

The foundations of any event are fragile, even war. There is no fact so pure that it can become definitive or put an end to History: what appears to be in flux might seem to proceed upon what seems to be in a state of permanence, but the invisible foundation that supports even the most important moments is the first to shake, and signs of change soon make their way into the material world.

As the weeks passed by it became clear that the war would have to come to an end. It was as if, we might say, obscenely, an aesthetic saturation had been reached: at first, the particular way in which the city had been fragmented by the conflict became a little irritating to see, and then, little by little, it became intolerable. Thus, the necessity of ending the war wasn't due to the return of some moral imperative or the recurrence of old resolutions: it was only that the repetition of its images had become excessive; the intense, fearful excitement people felt on seeing a corpse had now waned; explicit violence had abandoned its central place in narratives and had become integrated, now in an objective, neutral way, into written reports. The way people said "one more" while standing in front of a corpse had become more indicative of violence than the corpses themselves—lying crumpled in the street, mere matter divested of any trace of that humanity which had now disappeared in the same instantaneous and mysterious way that it had first arrived, in the midst of the person's family, on the day it was born. The desire for war was thus demolished, day after day, by this purely verbal construction, by this phrase that only existed in the world of language, without any visible connections to the world of objects: "One more." It was this "one more" that was going to end the war. Since the war had just been repeating itself for months, this feeling of "I've seen it all already" began to hold sway over even the most naïve and least clever people in the city.

The war, when it first arrived, had quickly become the only topic of conversation, and it was inserted into every form of human excitation, so to speak, populating the cities—even those intimate, private excitations shared by a man and his wife were dominated by this seemingly global form of excitation, by the excitation of the entire country. And for that reason the war was welcomed as a stimulating surprise, there's no other way to describe it, something that brought fear and obvious suffering, yes, but, in truth, it was hoped that these would remain tangential, indirect consequences. And, furthermore, the war satisfied a basic human need: intensity. Everything became more intense, from a simple glance at a map of the country—to find out where the soldiers were then marching—to the city streets, the shops, the houses, one's kitchen utensils: everything, from the universal to the miniscule, from the most public garden to the most personal chair, everything became more intense.

A mere knife in the kitchen possessed intensity. At the beginning of the war, whenever anyone picked up a household knife, for entirely peaceful purposes, fleeting energies would begin to flow, bestowing a certain new gravity upon this simple act and brutally amplifying one's otherwise monotonous or barren existence. However, this excitation faded with repetition—as might happen with any book or film that one has read or seen numerous times. How does one retain the anxiety of the moment when one is diving into the first page for the umpteenth time? What had taken place in the city, the streets, the houses, in the entire country, and with the kitchen knives too, what had taken place was something similar to aesthetic exhaustion; so similar that the two become confused. The war was starting to bore everyone; first those who were least involved, the ones who had the least to win or lose, and later, little by little, even those closest to its center, those who were stronger and, therefore, more ambitious. Ambition, although it was one of the last qualities to succumb, also became boring and, from a certain point onward, was also seen as a repetition: "I want more, one more time." And when tedium reached the strongest, those who could either win or lose the war, it marked the beginning of the end for all those things that had, for some time now, been repeating themselves to excess. Little by little, the signs became more pronounced, encroaching upon the realm of the visible, anxious to make their material entrance into the world. The end of the war was drawing near.

2

Over those years, the chaotic and unpredictable violence of the war had exhausted men. Simple, almost petty desires began to take on significant proportions. More and more each day, Margha Walser reminded her husband of the peaceful walks they used to take through the main city garden.

Certain people still had memories of a noiseless sky, one without airplanes. And there were memories too of something that had disappeared completely, at least in the public parts of the city: laziness. How long had men and women been deprived of the right to laziness, to moments devoid of useful action, and what's more: moments devoid of meaning.

For in wartime the meaningfulness of actions had become—as they say—inflamed, contaminated with something that quickly spread from one body to another, from men to women, from women to children, to the elderly, to the disabled: every single action had taken on meaning: What do you mean by that? What are you doing? Where are you going?

Laziness in wartime was either an obscenity—a lack of respect for those who were on the verge of dying or killing (one lowered ones eyes when faced with the victim or the perpetrators)—or else this action without action, laziness, was simply a manifestation of insanity: a retreat from the new norms.

Because actions full of import and meaning were the norm in wartime, and laziness was their inverse. Seeing someone who wasn't doing anything and didn't want to do anything would cause as much amazement and, probably, as much disapproval as seeing a lunatic in the middle of the city garden, in spring, repeating his brusque, impulsive movements: ripping flowers violently from the ground, stomping on flower beds, digging holes in the dirt with his fingers. During times of great intensity, someone who didn't know where he was headed or why he was doing what he was doing was a lunatic, for he was abstracted from the events around him. To delve into the world of abstraction in wartime—a period of absolutely concrete things, a period when matter and energy collide and battle one another—was the most violent of actions. Perhaps even the most immoral.

By the same token, Klober had already asked Walser this question: "Which is more immoral in times like these: to kill someone or to learn geometry?"

And Walser had never known how to respond.

CHAPTER XXV

1

The war is over! This authoritative phrase is published in the newspaper. People celebrate and hug their family members, inside their homes. Out on the street the handshakes are more vigorous, robust; friendships are reestablished, downcast eyes are raised a few inches: people now look at the upper half of other people's faces, and it's as if there is an implicit recommencement of all personal relationships. No one expresses it verbally; there is a general sense of embarrassment in friends who haven't spoken for years, but nevertheless a handshake between two men is able to accomplish what takes engineers months to do with destroyed houses: after all, a human feeling is a lighter and more easily repaired substance than stone, brick, or cement.

Certain habits are resumed after a few days. The butcher shop starts to open earlier; an obese man chops meat with renewed brutality. Fruits that haven't been seen for years begin to appear in the grocery stores, and money starts circulating, so much so that it almost seems that someone just started handing it out after the war ended.

There's a new excitement in the streets, a new vigor, a new will to do and to act, something very similar to what was felt during the first few weeks of the war. It may signify the opposite, but the energy at the root of this feeling is the same: organisms are always stimulated by change, are only stimulated by change.

Joseph Walser is excited, like all the city's inhabitants; he doesn't run through the streets, as some children are doing, but he does proceed quickly, with vigorous, resolute steps. He doesn't look like Joseph Walser.

"It's over," he says to himself, multiple times a day, for multiple days in a row; it seems that he can't tire of repeating it, for he doesn't yet think of it as a repetition, but rather as something surprising; he repeats: "It's over and I'm alive!" As if, strangely, being alive could be the end of something.

On one of those afternoons, after giving him a kiss, his wife, Margha, says, "We did it, Joseph!"

CHAPTER XXVI

1

Clairie's hands straightened up the small objects on the table for the third time. She moved them slightly to one side or another, just a few inches. She examined her face intently: her lips, her eyes, her nose, her hair. She straightened her neckline, searching for a way to project either indecision or inattention, leaving a little on display, but not too much. She knew that her breasts were still the chief source of interest in her body. She unfastened a button, pulled her shirt down lower, to the sides, seeking the perfect combination of clothing and breasts.

On that Sunday, the sun was behaving in a surprising way. From the early morning, the bright light portended a hotter day than had been forecast. It made Clairie happy. The sun had a positive effect on everyone, and in the afternoon she expected, at the end of a long wait, a visit from Mr. Walser.

As she waited, she went back into her bedroom and straightened the bedsheets again. Her body was occupied by a useful enthusiasm; she can't stop: she tidies up, cleans, straightens things up, and once again goes over to the mirror.

2

Meanwhile, people are strolling in the city garden, but in a dissolute way, as if bodies were substances that could evaporate. An imposed laziness. It's Sunday and the sky has behaved impeccably. Nary a cloud to be seen.

Distant friends embrace each other heartily and immediately shake hands. Nothing is blown about by the wind: it blows down from above, caressing men's faces gently and then moving along. Women can only sense it when they are quiet and motionless: the transitory wind.

The city garden brings the people's shoes to a halt, while four children transform into innumerable children as they play on the grass, because they never stop moving and are thus difficult to fix in one place. They play, and each marvel is cut short by another marvel; or at least they try to demonstrate that they're different from the adults. "When you see a body that constantly changes position, you are looking at a child," says someone. A definition of childhood proffered while this someone puts his hands in his pockets to look for a business card with his name on it. It's Sunday, but certain friendly contacts may prove useful in one's profession. Not everything that's pressing on Sunday is pressing on a weekday, but sometimes there are overlaps, even important ones.

The city infused with a dense happiness, a kind of controlled exultation that builds in layers, one on top of another.

Just outside the gardens, the city carries on apace with its memory well disposed toward forgiveness. There are only smiles; no one speaks of the past.

The important families of the city alter their routes in order to cross paths with each other.

3

Just over a month had passed since the war ended: Joseph Walser pushed his shoes aside with his foot. He was naked in front of Clairie.

Clairie had gained even more weight during that time, but she hadn't ceased to arouse Joseph. After some minor advances and retreats Walser was now in Clairie's house, naked, and exposing his erect penis. The lights had been turned off, at her request. Clairie gripped Joseph's penis and made vigorous movements. Joseph had already taken off her clothes and was now forcefully grabbing the ample breasts that hung over her stomach. Joseph Walser's fingers moved, one by one, down the length of her fat breasts, and at times contracted, forcefully gripping the woman's flesh. Walser's penis was already buried within her, disappearing into her copious pubic hair, forcefully penetrating into and pulling out of her vagina; his hands squeezed Clairie's fat legs, as well as the sides of her buttocks. Walser concentrated on the movements of his penis, penetrating and pulling out, and, more aroused every minute, he had started to pull her hair forcefully when he suddenly felt as if he'd been pushed backwards. Clairie was pushing him!

"Stop, please!" she said. "Turn on the lights."

Walser stood motionless.

"I'm sorry Mr. Walser," said Clairie. "It's your finger. I can't get it out of my mind!"

CHAPTER XXVII

1

Time had passed.

Two days earlier Joseph Walser had received an odd request from Klober, asking to meet him at the factory.

It was Sunday night, and he'd promised Clairie that he would stop by her house, and his wife, Margha, was also waiting for him so they could go for a stroll. The day was a fine one. The factory, empty.

He entered through the front gate, walked across a small patio, walked up a set of exterior stairs, and, already inside one of the factory buildings—the building where he used to work in the years before the accident with his machine—he started walking down a dozen stairs. A feeling of confusion and a certain fear materialized inside of Walser: he could hear the roar of the machines at work below. How was it possible? It was Sunday, nobody was working, and the factory seemed empty.

Foreman Klober's office. Same as ever. The door was open. Walser went in.

"My dear Walser, how nice it is to see you."

Klober extended his right hand to Walser, who responded in kind with his right hand.

"Don't take this the wrong way, but, my, how I've missed the touch of your hand! Its absence made my own hand itch. My dear fellow, let me say this right away, let me repeat it: I've missed your hand! You abandoned us, you know, my dear Walser? You went off to some other building and left us here all alone with the machines. You've already noticed it: can you hear them? They're all running. Exactly. They run on Sundays. All of them. I turned them on, isn't that extraordinary? The motors are running on Sunday. But I haven't called you here to talk about the indolence of some of these apparatuses. My dear Walser, wouldn't you like to sit down? No? All right, very well, standing, my dear sir, that's fine, you're more imposing that way. Okay, dear Walser, I would first like to shut the door, we wouldn't want to be interrupted, and you never know what will happen on Sunday. I'm going to lock it with this key, if you don't mind, so we can be certain we won't be interrupted. Here's the key, don't worry, I'll set it here close to you, right here, you see, within arm's reach. Very good.

"My dear Walser, you must be frightened, I know you. You are not a man who could be characterized as excessively courageous. You have never found yourself under attack by a single excess—if I may put it that way. You are what we could call a quiet man, Joseph, my friend, and I admire you for it. You know how to parcel out your energy, you've always known. Perhaps you know it in a way with which no machine could ever compete. You don't waste time, my dear fellow, you possess something that could be called an 'instinct of utility,' an instinct that allows you to distance yourself, precisely, from waste, from excess. You're a very precise man, Walser, and you should take this brief introduction as the expression of a fond weakness on your friend Klober's part: I am, in fact, happy to see you again. To talk to you again, and with plenty of time to spare, no rush. You are a man who listens, Joseph Walser, and it's not by chance that women must think of you as a valued confidant.

"But I can tell that you're afraid. Don't be silly, are we friends or not? How many years has it been? Many, maybe you'd say too many, since those years are evidence of the obvious fact that we're both getting older. But the startling thing is that I look at you and still see the same young man who first started working with our machines. A hard worker. Can you hear the noise? Listen.

"Wonderful, isn't it? The machines. All right then, prick up your ears. Now tell me, can you hear the sound of your own machine? Can you? There are many, I know, they're all running, and all by themselves, which is just absurd, but, after all, today is Sunday, and anything goes, we've been at peace for years and we're in need of some kind of amusement, some novelty, some kind of surprise. But listen. See if you can ferret out your own machine. Do you remember it? It took your finger, which seemed like a tragedy at the time, I remember it well, but look at you now. You're still going on, still moving forward, you know? I look at you and see that same young man, with the same judiciousness and the same exactitude.

And always such a good listener. My, how well you listen to other men! My dear Walser, you should be awarded a medal just for how well you listen to other men. I know that you didn't take part in the war, you were right to stay away from it, just like me, you could say. Such affairs aren't for people like us. I know that you stayed away from the weapons and that you aren't exactly a hero, but if it were up to me, the country would award you a medal tomorrow. You really listen to men. And that's a rare thing. But now listen to the machines as well, make an effort. See if you can listen to them as intently as you're listening to me right now; see if you can separate the noise they're making into individual, distinct words, and see if you can give this noise meaning, an exact meaning, just as you do with the words I am speaking. Yes, prick up your ears, as they say, my dear Walser, it's time to learn to listen to the machines.

"But I didn't call you here, on a Sunday, in the afternoon, on a sunny day during which you should be, along with the rest of the city, strolling in the park with your wife, with your amazing, steadfast wife, your faithful wife, and I say that without a hint of irony, I know what I'm talking about, she will never leave you; but as I was saying, I didn't call you here, depriving you of the sun and the park, to talk to you about machines; my dear friend, I called you here because I want to talk about myself, me: Klober, a simple inhabitant of this city, the foreman of one unit of one of the factories in the empire of Leo Vast, which is led these days by a beautiful woman, about whom they say shocking things, but also wonderful things, as befits the characters of the mighty. But, my dear Walser, we're on a different floor here. We're below them. This is my office. How many years has it been? Fifteen, twenty? They always kept me down below, close to the machines, so I wouldn't forget the warmth of their humming motors. Do you know that I still have never seen Leo Vast's widow, not even once? Not once. And, just between you and me, they say she's nice to look at. But what can we do, my friend and I? Here we are down below. We get our kicks with prostitutes. You, my dear Walser, more fortunate than me, sometimes sleep with poor Clairie, who's getting fatter by the week: indeed, you chose well. I can see that you like large women and I can't help but agree with you on that score. They're the ones who appreciate men the most, the ones that hold tightest to men. Life is tragic, my dear fellow, life is absolutely physical, have you noticed?

"It's when you have a physical defect like you, my friend, or when you are obese, that you realize that life is completely physical and that there is nothing else to it. That there's no such thing as a spirit, Joseph. There isn't a single drop of spirit among the living: obese women hold tight to men and never let them go, because they know that they'll probably never have another, and they hate that likelihood: the likelihood that they'll never have another. Clairie isn't holding on to you, my dear Walser, because she's madly in love with you, she's holding on to you because she would hate to be alone.

"What was it like to chase after a widow like that, Joseph, my friend? Only you would have done it. Do you know what they call her in the factory? Simply: 'the stupid fatty.' Isn't it excellent, as a summary, as a method of synthesis: 'the stupid fatty'? Do whatever you want with her. Try out weird things with her, my friend, I heartily advise you to do it. She might complain, but don't pay attention, women of her caliber only pretend to be offended. It's a survival instinct: they pretend to be offended. But they cannot refuse.

"But I want to show you something. I have it here in the drawer. Look, it's pretty, isn't it? A gun. And it's loaded.

"I want to talk about myself, my dear fellow, as I've already told you, that's the reason I called you here, to talk about myself; and because you're a good listener. All right then, I brought with me the necessary instrument for use in talking about myself: a pistol, an excellent pistol, a modern pistol, a loaded pistol, a pistol that has within it two deaths. That's just a figure of speech, don't be frightened, it has two deaths within it because it has two bullets: one for you and one for me, arithmetically speaking. But don't be frightened, don't be ridiculous, not now; I'm just using that as an example.

"Are you frightened? Oh, my dear friend, that was just a gunshot. Don't tell me you don't recognize that sound. After so many years of war, that sound still frightens you? That's extraordinary. You, my dear Walser, surprise me, you still surprise me. You're still carrying on with a naïveté that is absolutely remarkable. Everything is new to you. You're made of different stuff, you're from a different world, you're from a different century. All right then, my dear sir, you know that I'm not like that. Know that for me, in fact, the idea of putting a bullet in my head has crossed my mind many times. Have you ever heard of such a thing? Klober the foreman, Klober the foreman wants to put a bullet in his head? That's absurd, you'll say, in your immense naïveté. That may be: but a day doesn't pass that I don't think about putting a bullet in my head. In one side, out the other: a bullet in my very own head. But look here, don't get frightened because of me. I still haven't decided anything, I'm here to talk to you because I still haven't decided. That's why I called you, I know that you're a good listener, an extraordinary listener, and knowing that I knew it wouldn't be a mistake to bring you here, on a sunny Sunday, making you leave your faithful wife, and your beautiful lover, thus leaving two forlorn women behind on Sunday, a crucial day for hatred, a day on which hatred is in urgent need of parks and nice weather, of idle strolls; it's like this: I wouldn't rob you of all the happiness out there just to get you to witness my suicide. It would be an affront to your finest quality, that of being a good listener, if I were to call you just to watch me do it. So, I'll tell you something right away to ease your worries about my health. Well then, this gun now only has one bullet, the other was wasted, if we want to think of it that way; I fired off to the side; I missed, my dear Walser. I now have a single bullet in this pistol: it won't do for two people, it's easy to do the math, and I'll say that it has drastically reduced the probability of one of us dying, here, in this room. But I'm going to include you in this game, Walser, my friend—perhaps a little too early. Nevertheless, I want you to realize something: the war ended some time ago; so, my dear Walser, you are looking at a man who has never killed anyone. Can you believe it? Believe it, please, I beg of you. Here we are, locked in here, there's no one nearby, the machines are all running and I would never lie to you about such an important matter: yes, I may have betrayed a man at one time or another—I know that some were perhaps shot because of what I did or, at least, because of a sudden loss of memory on my part—but who isn't guilty of that? And you, Joseph, know very well what I'm talking about. Although you distanced yourself from these matters, you've also got something of a résumé in this regard, don't be so modest. But as I was saying: I have never killed a man. I've never aimed a gun. The substance of which the human body is constructed even nauseates me a little, I have to admit. The substance of the human body is much too inexplicable to me, and as such, I repeat, I cannot help but feel a little nauseated by men. Nothing excessive, of course: here I am, to this very day, having never shed blood, carrying on in my job, carrying on as Klober the foreman.

"But the hour is drawing nigh. I'm not going to ask you to shoot me, for a number of reasons. You're a peaceful man, no doubt about it; forcing you to shoot me would be an act of violence against you. Your hands worry me as well. Let's be frank: you're a disabled man. You have a grotesque hand: missing its index finger, with a hideous swelling in the palm. I must admit that the first time I shook your hand after the accident it gave me goose bumps; I, who have seen so much worse than that. Perhaps because you're my friend, who knows? It's a minor defect, almost imperceptible, almost invisible, I'd say. Just one finger, a few inches, if we want to be precise about it, if we want to be obscene about it. Allow me a moment of levity, Walser, my friend, don't be offended. These are my last moments of levity, and someone who's dying has a right to one last dance. But I was saying that your hands worry me: that's another reason I won't hand the gun over to you. If you were to shoot me with your left hand, I would be offended: no one should kill a man with his weak hand. But you, Joseph, have two weak hands, and that's what worries me. Honestly, it's a small defect, the one you have, confined to the index finger on your right hand. But do you know what that finger is? It's the finger that pulls the trigger, the finger that's essential for shooting: it's the finger—please excuse these final embellishments—but it is, indeed, the finger that's essential for killing. That's the one, there isn't another one that can be the crux, the medulla, to use that beautiful word, aside from the finger you no longer have. It would be rude to insist that you shoot me with your deformed hand. I would be highlighting your defect, that absence there. It wouldn't be the right thing for me to do. For that reason, I'll be the one who shoots. I would have liked for it to be you, Walser, I say that in all sincerity. To be killed by another human being would make more sense, it would be more appropriate for this century. But no, all I want is for you to see me: it's the most just and least offensive way for the both of us. Joseph Walser, my friend: your index finger was never missed so sorely as it is today. A damned amputation, my friend. And take note of the way these machines are, the way your machine is: look at what it took from you. It could have taken thousands of different things from your body, but it only took one, an apparently laughable one: your index finger.

"But don't lose the historical perspective. Even when you're inside an office, under lock and key—don't forget about the key, it's right here—but, as I was saying, even locked in an office, feeling too hot, and with the roar of the machines outside the door, even here, in this situation, we must not forget about History. And, my friend, your machine could hardly have been more precise than it was: in the middle of a war, what did it do to you, what did your machine do? Merely this: it took from you your most useful finger, the one that shoots, the finger that performs a final contraction just before someone in front of you disappears. The machines were mocking you, my dear fellow. We should be wary of the machines, I've told you that before. Their malice is far too precise. We'll never be able to achieve anything like it, ourselves.

"I'm going to put, then, a bullet precisely in the middle of my head, I'm going to insert a detail into it, but an outside detail, a metal one. And then, perhaps, dear Joseph, you'll be able to salvage it for your collection. What do you think?

"What an excellent word: medulla! That which is in the middle; and the head is in the middle, you see? Remember what I told you about the head being on top of the body? But no: in fact, it's in the middle after all.

"But enough of that, I thank you for listening to me so attentively, once again. I'm your friend, I hope that you finally realize that. You deserve to live, Walser, and I don't know of a better thing to say to a man; I don't know of a more just thing to say: you deserve to live.

"But let's hurry to fulfill our duties. We shouldn't slow down the tempo just because it's Sunday. Dear friend, look at these dice, let's roll them, what do you think? Two dice, you know them well. I always heard you were good player. I want to play! Let's play together. We've never played together, have we?

"You all always thought of me as someone you wouldn't want to play such games with, an undesirable. And you were right. I was never exactly efficient at joining in the games of others. That might seem like an odd way to put it, but it's precisely what we're talking about: being competent or not. And I, Joseph Walser, my friend, was never competent at games or diversions.

"But we've been here too long. I'm going to roll the dice, and you, my friend, will roll them next. I have a bullet in this gun: it's going to go into the head of the one who loses. It's simple. What do you think? It's a game. Excellent, isn't it? A double pastime.

"But you must not be afraid, dear Walser, you're already starting to fidget too much. Don't force me to violate the rules, as well as my own desire. Please, calm down, sit down! There you go. You're the dice player, not me. I'm certainly going to lose.

"Very good. Let's be reasonable, that's better. Are we ready to play? Here go my dice. There they go. Stop! What do we have here? A four and a three? Not bad for a non-player. What do you think, Walser, think you can do better? We could say that this four plus this three leaves some possibilities open for you. However, from a purely statistical point of view, I would be tempted to say that you, my friend, are now closer to taking the one bullet that's left in this gun—which, to be completely honest, I don't want to happen. But I'm talking to you about statistics in the middle of a game, which is quite absurd. Roll, my friend, it's your turn. Pick up the dice, there you go. It's your turn now. Please, toss them. There you go. Roll."

FROM THE NOTEBOOKS OF GONÇALO M. TAVARES | 8

GONÇALO M. TAVARES was born in 1970. He has published numerous books since 2001 and has been awarded an impressive number of literary prizes in a very short time, including the Saramago Prize in 2005 and the Fernando Namora Prize in 2011.

RHETT MCNEIL has translated work by Machado de Assis, António Lobo Antunes, Gonçalo M. Tavares, and A. G. Porta.

PETROS ABATZOGLOU, *What Does Mrs. Freeman Want?*
MICHAL AJVAZ, *The Golden Age.*
The Other City.
PIERRE ALBERT-BIROT, *Grabinoulor.*
YUZ ALESHKOVSKY, *Kangaroo.*
FELIPE ALFAU, *Chromos.*
Locos.
JOÃO ALMINO, *The Book of Emotions.*
IVAN ÂNGELO, *The Celebration.*
The Tower of Glass.
DAVID ANTIN, *Talking.*
ANTÓNIO LOBO ANTUNES,
Knowledge of Hell.
The Splendor of Portugal.
ALAIN ARIAS-MISSON, *Theatre of Incest.*
IFTIKHAR ARIF AND WAQAS KHWAJA, EDS.,
Modern Poetry of Pakistan.
JOHN ASHBERY AND JAMES SCHUYLER,
A Nest of Ninnies.
ROBERT ASHLEY, *Perfect Lives.*
GABRIELA AVIGUR-ROTEM, *Heatwave and Crazy Birds.*
HEIMRAD BÄCKER, *transcript.*
DJUNA BARNES, *Ladies Almanack.*
Ryder.
JOHN BARTH, *LETTERS.*
Sabbatical.
DONALD BARTHELME, *The King.*
Paradise.
SVETISLAV BASARA, *Chinese Letter.*
RENÉ BELLETTO, *Dying.*
MARK BINELLI, *Sacco and Vanzetti Must Die!*
ANDREI BITOV, *Pushkin House.*
ANDREJ BLATNIK, *You Do Understand.*
LOUIS PAUL BOON, *Chapel Road.*
My Little War.
Summer in Termuren.
ROGER BOYLAN, *Killoyle.*
IGNÁCIO DE LOYOLA BRANDÃO,
Anonymous Celebrity.
The Good-Bye Angel.
Teeth under the Sun.
Zero.
BONNIE BREMSER,
Troia: Mexican Memoirs.
CHRISTINE BROOKE-ROSE, *Amalgamemnon.*
BRIGID BROPHY, *In Transit.*
MEREDITH BROSNAN, *Mr. Dynamite.*
GERALD L. BRUNS, *Modern Poetry and the Idea of Language.*
EVGENY BUNIMOVICH AND J. KATES, EDS.,
Contemporary Russian Poetry: An Anthology.
GABRIELLE BURTON, *Heartbreak Hotel.*
MICHEL BUTOR, *Degrees.*
Mobile.
Portrait of the Artist as a Young Ape.
G. CABRERA INFANTE, *Infante's Inferno.*
Three Trapped Tigers.
JULIETA CAMPOS,
The Fear of Losing Eurydice.
ANNE CARSON, *Eros the Bittersweet.*
ORLY CASTEL-BLOOM, *Dolly City.*
CAMILO JOSÉ CELA, *Christ versus Arizona.*
The Family of Pascual Duarte.
The Hive.
LOUIS-FERDINAND CÉLINE, *Castle to Castle.*
Conversations with Professor Y.
London Bridge.

Normance.
North.
Rigadoon.
HUGO CHARTERIS, *The Tide Is Right.*
JEROME CHARYN, *The Tar Baby.*
ERIC CHEVILLARD, *Demolishing Nisard.*
MARC CHOLODENKO, *Mordechai Schamz.*
JOSHUA COHEN, *Witz.*
EMILY HOLMES COLEMAN, *The Shutter of Snow.*
ROBERT COOVER, *A Night at the Movies.*
STANLEY CRAWFORD, *Log of the S.S. The Mrs Unguentine.*
Some Instructions to My Wife.
ROBERT CREELEY, *Collected Prose.*
RENÉ CREVEL, *Putting My Foot in It.*
RALPH CUSACK, *Cadenza.*
SUSAN DAITCH, *L.C.*
Storytown.
NICHOLAS DELBANCO,
The Count of Concord.
Sherbrookes.
NIGEL DENNIS, *Cards of Identity.*
PETER DIMOCK, *A Short Rhetoric for Leaving the Family.*
ARIEL DORFMAN, *Konfidenz.*
COLEMAN DOWELL,
The Houses of Children.
Island People.
Too Much Flesh and Jabez.
ARKADII DRAGOMOSHCHENKO, *Dust.*
RIKKI DUCORNET, *The Complete Butcher's Tales.*
The Fountains of Neptune.
The Jade Cabinet.
The One Marvelous Thing.
Phosphor in Dreamland.
The Stain.
The Word "Desire."
WILLIAM EASTLAKE, *The Bamboo Bed.*
Castle Keep.
Lyric of the Circle Heart.
JEAN ECHENOZ, *Chopin's Move.*
STANLEY ELKIN, *A Bad Man.*
Boswell: A Modern Comedy.
Criers and Kibitzers, Kibitzers and Criers.
The Dick Gibson Show.
The Franchiser.
George Mills.
The Living End.
The MacGuffin.
The Magic Kingdom.
Mrs. Ted Bliss.
The Rabbi of Lud.
Van Gogh's Room at Arles.
FRANÇOIS EMMANUEL, *Invitation to a Voyage.*
ANNIE ERNAUX, *Cleaned Out.*
LAUREN FAIRBANKS, *Muzzle Thyself.*
Sister Carrie.
LESLIE A. FIEDLER, *Love and Death in the American Novel.*
JUAN FILLOY, *Op Oloop.*
GUSTAVE FLAUBERT, *Bouvard and Pécuchet.*
KASS FLEISHER, *Talking out of School.*
FORD MADOX FORD,
The March of Literature.
JON FOSSE, *Aliss at the Fire.*
Melancholy.
MAX FRISCH, *I'm Not Stiller.*

Man in the Holocene.
CARLOS FUENTES, *Christopher Unborn.*
Distant Relations.
Terra Nostra.
Where the Air Is Clear.
WILLIAM GADDIS, *J R.*
The Recognitions.
JANICE GALLOWAY, *Foreign Parts.*
The Trick Is to Keep Breathing.
WILLIAM H. GASS, *Cartesian Sonata
and Other Novellas.*
Finding a Form.
A Temple of Texts.
The Tunnel.
Willie Masters' Lonesome Wife.
GÉRARD GAVARRY, *Hoppla! 1 2 3.*
Making a Novel.
ETIENNE GILSON,
The Arts of the Beautiful.
Forms and Substances in the Arts.
C. S. GISCOMBE, *Giscome Road.*
Here.
Prairie Style.
DOUGLAS GLOVER, *Bad News of the Heart.*
The Enamoured Knight.
WITOLD GOMBROWICZ,
A Kind of Testament.
KAREN ELIZABETH GORDON,
The Red Shoes.
GEORGI GOSPODINOV, *Natural Novel.*
JUAN GOYTISOLO, *Count Julian.*
Exiled from Almost Everywhere.
Juan the Landless.
Makbara.
Marks of Identity.
PATRICK GRAINVILLE, *The Cave of Heaven.*
HENRY GREEN, *Back.*
Blindness.
Concluding.
Doting.
Nothing.
JACK GREEN, *Fire the Bastards!*
JIŘÍ GRUŠA, *The Questionnaire.*
GABRIEL GUDDING,
Rhode Island Notebook.
MELA HARTWIG, *Am I a Redundant
Human Being?*
JOHN HAWKES, *The Passion Artist.*
Whistlejacket.
ALEKSANDAR HEMON, ED.,
Best European Fiction.
AIDAN HIGGINS, *A Bestiary.*
Balcony of Europe.
Bornholm Night-Ferry.
Darkling Plain: Texts for the Air.
Flotsam and Jetsam.
Langrishe, Go Down.
Scenes from a Receding Past.
Windy Arbours.
KEIZO HINO, *Isle of Dreams.*
KAZUSHI HOSAKA, *Plainsong.*
ALDOUS HUXLEY, *Antic Hay.*
Crome Yellow.
Point Counter Point.
Those Barren Leaves.
Time Must Have a Stop.
NAOYUKI Ii, *The Shadow of a Blue Cat.*
MIKHAIL IOSSEL AND JEFF PARKER, EDS.,
*Amerika: Russian Writers View the
United States.*
DRAGO JANČAR, *The Galley Slave.*
GERT JONKE, *The Distant Sound.*

Geometric Regional Novel.
Homage to Czerny.
The System of Vienna.
JACQUES JOUET, *Mountain R.*
Savage.
Upstaged.
CHARLES JULIET, *Conversations with
Samuel Beckett and Bram van
Velde.*
MIEKO KANAI, *The Word Book.*
YORAM KANIUK, *Life on Sandpaper.*
HUGH KENNER, *The Counterfeiters.*
*Flaubert, Joyce and Beckett:
The Stoic Comedians.*
Joyce's Voices.
DANILO KIŠ, *Garden, Ashes.*
A Tomb for Boris Davidovich.
ANITA KONKKA, *A Fool's Paradise.*
GEORGE KONRÁD, *The City Builder.*
TADEUSZ KONWICKI, *A Minor Apocalypse.*
The Polish Complex.
MENIS KOUMANDAREAS, *Koula.*
ELAINE KRAF, *The Princess of 72nd Street.*
JIM KRUSOE, *Iceland.*
EWA KURYLUK, *Century 21.*
EMILIO LASCANO TEGUI, *On Elegance
While Sleeping.*
ERIC LAURRENT, *Do Not Touch.*
HERVÉ LE TELLIER, *The Sextine Chapel.*
*A Thousand Pearls (for a Thousand
Pennies)*
VIOLETTE LEDUC, *La Bâtarde.*
EDOUARD LEVÉ, *Autoportrait.*
Suicide.
SUZANNE JILL LEVINE, *The Subversive
Scribe: Translating Latin
American Fiction.*
DEBORAH LEVY, *Billy and Girl.*
*Pillow Talk in Europe and Other
Places.*
JOSÉ LEZAMA LIMA, *Paradiso.*
ROSA LIKSOM, *Dark Paradise.*
OSMAN LINS, *Avalovara.*
The Queen of the Prisons of Greece.
ALF MAC LOCHLAINN,
The Corpus in the Library.
Out of Focus.
RON LOEWINSOHN, *Magnetic Field(s).*
MINA LOY, *Stories and Essays of Mina Loy.*
BRIAN LYNCH, *The Winner of Sorrow.*
D. KEITH MANO, *Take Five.*
MICHELINE AHARONIAN MARCOM,
The Mirror in the Well.
BEN MARCUS,
The Age of Wire and String.
WALLACE MARKFIELD,
Teitlebaum's Window.
To an Early Grave.
DAVID MARKSON, *Reader's Block.*
Springer's Progress.
Wittgenstein's Mistress.
CAROLE MASO, *AVA.*
LADISLAV MATEJKA AND KRYSTYNA
POMORSKA, EDS.,
*Readings in Russian Poetics:
Formalist and Structuralist Views.*
HARRY MATHEWS,
*The Case of the Persevering Maltese:
Collected Essays.*
Cigarettes.
The Conversions.
The Human Country: New and

Martereau.
The Planetarium.
ARNO SCHMIDT, *Collected Novellas.*
  Collected Stories.
  Nobodaddy's Children.
  Two Novels.
ASAF SCHURR, *Motti.*
CHRISTINE SCHUTT, *Nightwork.*
GAIL SCOTT, *My Paris.*
DAMION SEARLS, *What We Were Doing*
  and Where We Were Going.
JUNE AKERS SEESE,
  Is This What Other Women Feel Too?
  What Waiting Really Means.
BERNARD SHARE, *Inish.*
  Transit.
AURELIE SHEEHAN,
  Jack Kerouac Is Pregnant.
VIKTOR SHKLOVSKY, *Bowstring.*
  Knight's Move.
  A Sentimental Journey:
    Memoirs 1917–1922.
  Energy of Delusion: A Book on Plot.
  Literature and Cinematography.
  Theory of Prose.
  Third Factory.
  Zoo, or Letters Not about Love.
CLAUDE SIMON, *The Invitation.*
PIERRE SINIAC, *The Collaborators.*
KJERSTI A. SKOMSVOLD, *The Faster I Walk,*
  the Smaller I Am.
JOSEF ŠKVORECKÝ, *The Engineer of*
  Human Souls.
GILBERT SORRENTINO,
  Aberration of Starlight.
  Blue Pastoral.
  Crystal Vision.
  Imaginative Qualities of Actual
    Things.
  Mulligan Stew.
  Pack of Lies.
  Red the Fiend.
  The Sky Changes.
  Something Said.
  Splendide-Hôtel.
  Steelwork.
  Under the Shadow.
W. M. SPACKMAN,
  The Complete Fiction.
ANDRZEJ STASIUK, *Dukla.*
  Fado.
GERTRUDE STEIN,
  Lucy Church Amiably.
  The Making of Americans.
  A Novel of Thank You.
LARS SVENDSEN, *A Philosophy of Evil.*
PIOTR SZEWC, *Annihilation.*
GONÇALO M. TAVARES, *Jerusalem.*
  Joseph Walser's Machine.
  Learning to Pray in the Age of
    Technique.
LUCIAN DAN TEODOROVICI,
  Our Circus Presents . . .
NIKANOR TERATOLOGEN, *Assisted Living.*
STEFAN THEMERSON, *Hobson's Island.*
  The Mystery of the Sardine.
  Tom Harris.
JOHN TOOMEY, *Sleepwalker.*
JEAN-PHILIPPE TOUSSAINT,
  The Bathroom.
  Camera.
  Monsieur.

Running Away.
Self-Portrait Abroad.
Television.
The Truth about Marie.
DUMITRU TSEPENEAG,
  Hotel Europa.
  The Necessary Marriage.
  Pigeon Post.
  Vain Art of the Fugue.
ESTHER TUSQUETS, *Stranded.*
DUBRAVKA UGRESIC,
  Lend Me Your Character.
  Thank You for Not Reading.
MATI UNT, *Brecht at Night.*
  Diary of a Blood Donor.
  Things in the Night.
ÁLVARO URIBE AND OLIVIA SEARS, EDS.,
  Best of Contemporary Mexican
    Fiction.
ELOY URROZ, *Friction.*
  The Obstacles.
LUISA VALENZUELA, *Dark Desires and*
  the Others.
  He Who Searches.
MARJA-LIISA VARTIO,
  The Parson's Widow.
PAUL VERHAEGHEN, *Omega Minor.*
AGLAJA VETERANYI, *Why the Child Is*
  Cooking in the Polenta.
BORIS VIAN, *Heartsnatcher.*
LLORENÇ VILLALONGA, *The Dolls' Room.*
ORNELA VORPSI, *The Country Where No*
  One Ever Dies.
AUSTRYN WAINHOUSE, *Hedyphagetica.*
PAUL WEST,
  Words for a Deaf Daughter & Gala.
CURTIS WHITE,
  America's Magic Mountain.
  The Idea of Home.
  Memories of My Father Watching TV.
  Monstrous Possibility: An Invitation
    to Literary Politics.
  Requiem.
DIANE WILLIAMS, *Excitability:*
  Selected Stories.
  Romancer Erector.
DOUGLAS WOOLF, *Wall to Wall.*
  Ya! & John-Juan.
JAY WRIGHT, *Polynomials and Pollen.*
  The Presentable Art of Reading
    Absence.
PHILIP WYLIE, *Generation of Vipers.*
MARGUERITE YOUNG, *Angel in the Forest.*
  Miss MacIntosh, My Darling.
REYOUNG, *Unbabbling.*
VLADO ŽABOT, *The Succubus.*
ZORAN ŽIVKOVIĆ, *Hidden Camera.*
LOUIS ZUKOFSKY, *Collected Fiction.*
VITOMIL ZUPAN, *Minuet for Guitar.*
SCOTT ZWIREN, *God Head.*